Odalisque

Odalisque

ALFRED DePEW

Dog Star Press
Vancouver, BC

Odalisque

Shakespeare's Sonnet 130 quoted on p. 39.

Excerpts from *le Refus Global*, found in Paul-Emile Borduas: *Ecrits/Writings 1942-1958* (Halifax: Press of the Nova Scotia College of Art and Design, 1978). Translated by François-Marc Gagnon and Dennis Young. Reprinted by permission.

Guillaume Apollinaire, excerpts from "The White Snow" ("*La blanche neige*," *Alcools*); "Moonlight" ("*Clair de Lune*," *Alcools*); and "*Vitam Impendere Amori*" ("To Threaten Life for Love"). Translated by A. S. Kline. Reprinted by Permission.

François Rabelais, *Le Quart Livre* quoted on p. 84.

ISBN: 978-0-9919939-8-7

Book and cover design by Nina Shoroplova
Font: Crimson Text

Printed in the United States of America

for Harry Faddis
who continues to guide me
with rigorous love
through every conceivable kind of terrain

and for William
healer—poet—priest

CONTENTS

PREFACE

This book was not my idea, which is to say it wasn't anything I was planning to write. In fact, I was eager to get back to a project I had set aside while writing *A Wedding Song for Poorer People*, which I had finished in New Mexico the summer of 2001. But *Odalisque* occurred to me instead, occurred *in* me as physical sensation, an unfolding dream that my body just couldn't shake.

Two months after I arrived home in Maine from New Mexico, a friend invited me to Quebec City for the first time. As we walked around town that first evening, everything seemed strangely familiar. I felt I knew this place. But not first-hand. I seemed to know it *through* someone else, and not the friend who was showing me around. Then I remembered a character I'd had in mind for some time—a woman's voice—the first few lines of a story, maybe—bold and sassy, in what seemed like a Brooklyn accent. A kind of updated version of Moll Flanders, the unrepentant prostitute.

In the days that followed, I learned more about this character. She wasn't from Brooklyn; she lived in Quebec City. I discovered which streets were familiar to her. I began to know her history, where she had come from, how she had made her living, who her lovers had been, what she had stood for. Not all at once, but gradually, in images, dreams, fragments of dialogue that I wrote down over the next five years as best I could in various notebooks—in hotel rooms, restaurants, the library, cafés, and any number of diners along the route I drove between Quebec City and Portland, Maine.

One day at the Musée national des beaux-arts, I discovered les Automatistes, and I knew that this character—by then her name was Thérèse—was somehow connected to them. In their 1948 manifesto, *Le Refus Global*, this group of painters and poets rejected the hegemony of the Catholic Church and the provincial government of Maurice Duplessis, as well as everything else that had served to oppress and restrain the soul of the Quebecois for generations. Shortly after it was published, the manifesto's author, painter Paul-Émile Borduas, was fired from his teaching job at the École du meuble in Montreal, and one of the signatories had her children taken away from her and put into foster care. Some of the group went into exile, choosing to live in France, including Canada's best known abstract painter, Jean-Paul Riopelle, who later divided his time between France and Quebec. Many believe that the manifesto announced the beginning of modern French Canada and that les Automatistes sowed the seeds of what later came to be known as the Quiet Revolution.

I knew Thérèse was connected to this group, but I didn't know how. They were in Montreal. Thérèse lived in Quebec City. I tried to persuade her to move, but she wouldn't even consider it. And then she showed me the link—the art school. She had modelled there, become friendly with the students who were about her age, and become lovers with one, Theo, who urged her to paint and introduced her to les Automatistes, whose method spoke to her intuition, her dreaming, and her own deepest impulses toward independence and autonomy.

In order to follow Thérèse, I had to keep moving in and out of a kind of dream state. I proceeded *à la dérive*, adrift, rudderless, without conscious intention, letting myself be led by this figure in my imagination. I stayed with the original impulses and promptings for as long as possible, but at some point I came up against the questions one always encounters when writing: Where is this leading? What does it mean? But in the context of *automatiste* methods, these were the wrong questions. They carried me too far afield from the images and scenes. The wild spirit I was tracking through the wilderness could vanish at any moment. More often than not, I had to remain very still and wait for her to approach.

Which is what one does with a dream. The busy mind of the ego, with its interpretive questions, must fall asleep so the psyche can do her work: producing non-rational, non-linear, amoral scenes and images, which at first glance seem nonsensical and absurd. And so we usually dismiss them. Until we can't. Thérèse is compelled to follow her dreaming without question or interpretation. In the process she records her impressions, desires, sensations, wounds, and memories. True to her *automatiste* ideas, she does not engage in analysis. Nothing in her seems to feel the need to sum up, explain, defend, apologize, or confess.

And so, like any other dreamer, we are left to form our own associations and responses.

May 2018, Vancouver, BC

Novembre. La saison de la mort, avant la neige. The season of death, before the snow. The trees along boulevard Saint-Cyrille, wrapped in burlap like religious statues in Lent. The Parliament grey against a grey sky, and everything still—until the rains come.

And the wind. Then stillness again.

This evening, I wander without destination.

I stop at the café on Saint-Jean, across from the shoe shop that used to be an undertaker's. As soon as it changed over, we all knew where the dress shoes came from. Nobody blamed Monsieur Benoit. After all, to bury perfectly good shoes during the war, when there were so many living feet in need of them to wear to weddings and christenings. Because weddings and christenings continued. The war couldn't stop them. In fact, it hastened them.

The war lent our lives an urgency, a sense that we may have only this moment—this heat. And so we must love now before we are called away to our death.

The moon tonight is low in the sky, further to the south than last month.

Large and astonishing.

Like the painting I worked on all morning, my hands trembling as I layered pale blue over darkness, clear water over sleep, like rain, or river water running over a black rock.

The smell of your body is still on my skin. I don't want to bathe. I want to linger with you, and so I order another cognac and go on writing.

James

Rose petals on the bed, as though we were ordinary lovers.

You pull a cloth over me, and I stand veiled in azure silk shot through with gold threads. You unveil, then veil me again—slowly. I lie on the bed as if under a shroud, candles lit all around, one votive light between my breasts. I'm afraid I'll burn but say nothing, remembering the gifts you often place between my breasts after love—chocolate truffles, stones smoothed by the river. I wait, perfectly still, breathing slowly and evenly so as not to overturn the flame at my heart, letting it burn steadily, steadily.

Sometimes it feels as if I die, and you bring me back to life again and again—my body grown light from hours of touch, floating, as if in the next wave of your hand, you could send me gliding across the room.

Circus magician.

Priest.

Only say the word and I shall be healed.

My legs wrapped around your waist, my back arched. You reach up, holding a chalice I cannot see, while new waves of sensation course up my spine, and my whole body shudders.

I'm a deaf-mute, or an angel with no earthly language, a tongue of fire with no sound. All of God's glorification—silent, shimmering in the air around us like green flame.

Oh James, if only I could have spoken this, or *you* could have. What an astonishing priest you would have been. Your church full of a fierce and relentless love that would open the world.

The night we met, you were acting as the Bishop's chauffeur. I looked over my shoulder at you as I led him upstairs. The only thing stronger than your indignation was your curiosity—I could see it in your face. I liked you for it—liked you for them both, actually.

For the struggle between those two impulses.

Your ambition—a cool calculation at odds with your heat.

So English.

And, of course, I am vain.

I liked your desire for me, mingled—as it so often was—with contempt.

Even then, I'd grown used to that in men.

How I wanted to stay there, to turn and face you, but I was strangely shy, even as I escorted the Bishop upstairs to my bed. Thinking of you downstairs made me laugh, which delighted the Bishop, the laugh itself. He didn't suspect its source. You in your cheap scratchy suit, holding your fedora

between your knees, sitting on the edge of a red velvet arm-
chair that was made to lean back into.

You were twenty-one, perhaps twenty-two. Oh! The
look of misery on your face when we came back downstairs.
I felt like saying, "Welcome to the World, my little brother,"
though I was even younger than you. How worldly-wise I felt
at seventeen; *une vraie femme du monde* I must have seemed to
you. I was so proud. I'd been fighting long and hard for just
that, though I couldn't have known it until I caught sight of
it in your face. I had arrived.

You were to drive the Bishop back to the parish house.
It may have even been your first day on the job. I ached for
you, but only a little. The rest was shameless pride, triumph
even, that I knew so much more than an Englishman—well,
an English Canadian—and a clergyman at that.

This I confess, Father. My pride. My knowledge of the
world. Knowing even then what you would never know with
all your books. I grew dizzy wanting to tell you. Boastful.
What a terrible pleasure. What a source of ferocious pain. I
had to keep so much to myself—to protect others. You were,
in some ways, the enemy, an Anglican, which has made my
suffering all the more delicious.

The first time we're alone together is at dawn, by a lake. The
musky smell of mud between the water's edge and grass. We
arrive at the same time. We do not speak. My feet are bare.
The dew is almost cold. I take off my clothes, fold them on
a dry rock, and enter the water swiftly. It takes a moment
before I reach the depth I want. I turn back and you are not
yet out of your trousers, hopping on one foot. I want to
laugh at you but decide to hold the silence, which is huge all
around us. You enter the water at a run, splashing, waving
your arms for balance, then dive and skim along the surface,

making a graceful wake. We swim and keep swimming until we reach the roots and rocks on the other side and then turn back, return, hand over hand, in rhythm, to the first shore. We half walk, half crawl back out of the water and dress in silence, turned away from one another. We part and don't see each other again until breakfast an hour later.

We've come away with the Bishop. Well, I have come away with him. You have driven us to the house he's borrowed on a lake in the Laurentians above Baie-St-Paul. He likes you. He trusts you. He seems to be bringing you along, preparing you to one day *be* the Bishop. He is fatherly toward us both, attending to my education, helping you along with your career, your vocation. And here we are together in roles that are indistinct, enjoying a kind of democracy this weekend. You are both driver and colleague. I am both mistress and daughter. Between the three of us there seems to be a great open friendship that is nonetheless full of secrets. We make no reference to the fact that the Bishop and I are sleeping together, nor do we (you and I) acknowledge what we both already know—that we will, in fact, become lovers. It is the first time we have seen each other naked. We have not yet touched. The innocence of this excites us both.

"And what did you dream, *Monseigneur*?" I ask as I pass the marmalade to the Bishop.

"I'm quite sure I don't know, my dear. You don't put much stock in dreams, do you?"

"*Mais oui, certainement*! We all tell our dreams at the house and sometimes more than one of us dreams the same dream, the way we sometimes get our monthlies at the same time." It comes out of my mouth before I realize what I've said. "*Excusez-moi, Monseigneur.*"

He smiles and shakes his head and goes on applying the marmalade to his toast.

"And you, *monsieur*. What did you dream?"

"I'm afraid I don't dream."

"Dr. Freud would insist that you do," says the Bishop.

"Well, if I do, I certainly don't remember."

"I dreamt I swam to the other side of the lake, and the water became gold as the sun rose. And there was someone swimming alongside me, and birds calling to one another in the trees."

I sense the danger I have put you in, and for a moment I'm sorry. But only for a moment.

"Well then, James, shall we have a go at psychoanalysis, then? The lake, for example. How do you interpret the lake?"

"I'm afraid I haven't a clue."

I notice the Bishop's affection for you, how he invites you to open up. And I notice for the first time, how often you begin a sentence with "I'm afraid."

When we find ourselves at the lake again, it is weeks later. We are alone. You tell the Bishop you are going to see family, a cousin, and he kindly offers you his car and ration cards for gas. High summer. I wear a cotton dress the colour of lemons, with spaghetti straps, sandals on my feet. You wear linen trousers and a white shirt. When the sun hits us we are ablaze with light, blinding, invisible to the ordinary human eye. It is getting to be mid-afternoon by the time we reach a place secluded enough. Not the place where we entered the water before. Here, we are in a thicket of spruce trees, a carpet of needles on the forest floor. Ferns and a small grassy place by the water, not a beach. Others have been here before us. Not that they've left anything behind. It's the small cleared-away places, made smooth through repetition, that give the impression of a room, where one can sit or lie down.

We arrive, and it strikes me that you've been here before —with another girl, perhaps. (I'm hardly in a position to criticize.) Or have we simply come upon this spot? You are nervous enough to make me think you're still a virgin, and yet once we are in the water and you have lifted me onto you I can't believe this is your first time. I am wedged between the exposed roots of a tree, my back against the cool mossy trunk. I'm relieved to be taken, simply and furiously. In water. Like birth. Like drowning. You thrust me up out of the water, and we sink back in again slowly. Rising and sinking. Our torsos above water, our legs entwined below the surface. All without a word.

The awkwardness afterwards makes me think again it may be your first time after all. Or it is the situation. We are without the Bishop, the first thing we have in common. Now there is this. And before that our longing. We must keep this secret. It will be the first I keep from *Monseigneur*, the first of a string growing ever longer even after I leave the house and he sets me up in an apartment of my own. And a studio. My "studies," as he calls them, interest him. He tries to be a fan of modern art, though he claims to understand nothing about it. Not that he would try to come between us, I think. It's that we mustn't risk his finding out. And we know this without speaking it. There is entirely too much in the beginning that we know or think we know without speaking.

For you and I, James, there is no future—only a continuous present moment, stolen from the life you live where there is a future. And if, as the years roll on, the future happens to intrude, you say, "Perhaps it would be best if we didn't..."

But you are safe. There is no place for us in the future. "This" cannot "make sense," as you put it. "This" that we are now. Here in this room in the crooked house in the *ruelle,* where you come to find relief—from your daily woes, hungers, grief, uncertainties, betrayal, and your gnawing sense of guilt.

None of that matters when we close the door and seize the moment we do have—now.

Where did I go? Where did you take me, James? And why are you crying? Your touch pushed me so far beyond—but where is this? Your head rises from between my legs, wet with my sex and your tears. Why are you crying? Have I given birth to you? I am so still. Am I dead? Is that why you're crying? Did I forget to bring you along? Your touch is here on my body. Your hands. I am warm. I shudder. I am still living. But how far beyond I am. This must be what it's like. Somewhat. Dying. This awareness of being beyond all who are left behind, weeping.

Was it back to Theo, then? Is that where I swam—back, up, forward in time? Not Theo as such. Not an image or even a memory of him. But Theo as he now lives sometimes in my body, that transcendent pleasure dream-state.

You rise and dress, compose yourself, and go home. I leave the house and find myself at Mass, just in time, kneeling, soaring. I can barely keep my balance. I might ascend into Heaven right then and there. I find myself in Mass *à la dérive*, or does God guide me there, not for penance, but to remember to give thanks for this ecstasy, this transcendence, this love—grace moving through my body, moving you to tears and pushing me—*beyond*, propelled up toward the surface of something, as one rises in water not of one's own volition, an opposite kind of gravitational pull. Then swimming—toward breath, and some greater brightness.

I did not wilfully turn my mind from you, beloved; it turned itself, spiralled up through something like memory, but in the future. And there you were, weeping, as if I'd died. Or because you knew you couldn't follow me. Or for some other reason I can never know. And couldn't ask about. Because then I'd have had to admit my betrayal.

Once the war is over, the Bishop finds you a wife. And because the Bishop is a man of the world, he brings your bride-to-be to me to instruct her in the art of loving you.

Who should know better than I?

He escorts her to the house on a Monday. I find her sitting in one of the red chairs when I enter the parlour. She wears a brown skirt, a beige silk blouse, and a tweed jacket. Expensive and surprisingly stylish for a schoolteacher. Her *cloche* is becoming. Her face is lovely; she is actually quite beautiful. I am at once pleased for you and jealous.

I admire her courage for coming.

I bow to the Bishop and step toward her to shake her hand.

She rises to greet me. A gesture of respect I shall never forget.

"Helen, this is Thérèse."

"How do you do?" she says.

"Enchantée, mademoiselle."

Instinct tells me that it's best to keep our worlds as far apart as possible. It will be easier for her if I remain different. As if we were not both Canadian women of about the same age. There is the question of class. And race. Not to mention profession.

I remain "other" simply by speaking French.

I see that she's both relieved and concerned.

"Don't worry. My English is quite good," I say to reassure her.

The Bishop opens his mouth to say something, then thinks better of it. I half think that he's about to boast about my knowledge of Wordsworth, so that suddenly we all three of us share something in common besides you, whom we don't mention.

But that would not do.

So he turns to me and says, "I've explained everything to Helen."

And to Helen, "I leave you in most capable hands."

Her gaze is so candid, her smile so genuine, that I am completely disarmed, and a little in love with her already.

Our lessons begin slowly. I am a model of delicacy and tact.

I undress her, hang her skirt and blouse in the armoire, fold her underthings carefully, and place them on a chair.

I touch her lightly, all over. She shivers. I touch her more firmly, massaging her shoulders, her neck.

I smooth her hair, her face with a tenderness that surprises us both.

Though we are the same age, I have the wisdom and experience of a much older woman. I have grown skilled, adept, and tactful under Arienne's tutelage.

I feel unspeakably old. Or this feels ancient.

We are in the temple of Aphrodite. I am initiating your future wife to the pleasures of her own body.

Your body, she must discover for herself.

It is enough this first time to touch her lightly, firmly, all over, to gauge her response.

"You must tell me what gives you pleasure and what doesn't."

Just before I reach the mound of fur below her belly, she stops my hand and looks up at me, frightened.

I rest where I am and let her guide my hand further until I gently cup her vulva.

We barely speak during this first lesson.

I smile and kiss her forehead.

She rises and dresses carefully. She is fastidious about her appearance, not vain, but in the way a woman aware of her own beauty takes time to arrange herself.

I show her downstairs, where we sit for a time with the Bishop and drink tea.

It is a measure of his tact that there is no awkwardness at all between the three of us.

And this is how I meet the woman who will love you as only I have loved you until now.

The lessons continue. Each Monday, because the house is closed to regular patrons, the Bishop's car delivers Helen just after lunch and then comes to call for her at four. Of course, you are no longer the Bishop's driver. You are now the rector of a church in Sillery with a parsonage, and soon Helen will join you there.

You don't visit during these months, which is as it should be. And I wonder if I shall ever see you again. Of course, we've had no conversation about Helen or what will become of us after your marriage to her. All business has been conducted through the Bishop, perhaps without your knowing about it.

I have already prepared the bridegroom.

Now I must prepare the bride.

She learns quickly and well—is, in fact, eager to learn more.

I dress her in gowns and outlandish hats. We are two girls playing with grandmother's old clothes. She assumes each pose with new daring. Now a harlot. Now an English lady in jodhpurs, boots, and a riding crop!

How we laugh!

I dress and undress her, tenderly, faithfully. I am by turns a serving maid and love's High Priestess.

Helen's trust in me grows, as does our affection for one another, yet it is pleasure itself that breaks through the last bounds of her strict upbringing and ignorance. She is relieved and overjoyed.

Who knows? Had the world been different, we might have been friends, after a fashion.

But when she leaves me for the last time and turns to wave before stepping into the Bishop's car, I know I won't see her again. Until your funeral years later.

So guileless is Helen that she sends me an invitation to your wedding. I send my sincerest regrets with a small, framed postcard of Botticelli's *Birth of Venus*.

"For your dressing table," I write. "As a daily reminder."

To which she responds in her neat, squarish hand, "Only you know how much this means to me. Thank you from the bottom of my heart—for *everything*."

When she leaves for the last time, it occurs to me that you will disappear as well for a period of weeks or months. But the months stretch into years without a word from you.

One night a terrible wind from the north rocks the trees, sucks the heat from the room, out the window, and I remember how your hands burned me.

I want to paint you, your strong back against the sky, seated on the grass—with an isthmus or peninsula jutting into the water you gaze out upon. Not landscape, as such. But the feeling of your body against it, as part of it.

I stare at a vase of purple tulips—amethyst. A greenish

light on them through the cloth over the window. Light emanating from their white hearts. I remember you touching each of my breasts with a tulip as I nodded off. When I opened my eyes, you were kneeling by the bedside in prayer. When you looked at me, your eyes were full of tears. I was so relieved to see you. I was weary and heavy with pleasure. I placed my hands on my ovaries. You called my belly a melon, my breasts full of milk and honey—the boundless love of God, you said, as though I were carrying your child. You placed your lips just so—to suck the sweetness from my navel, you said. I was so grateful to have you for these moments you stole from your other life.

In our time together we created and carried something forward—somehow doing God's work in the world. From the pulpit, you may well have condemned me, but here, kneeling beside my bed, you venerated me.

We were like the early Christians, pure and humble in our lack of dogma. We invented our acts of devotion, inspired in the moment. Even our disagreements, our wounds and betrayals, were sacred. In the rooms we visited together, we were stripped of our worldly identities, so our loving could include the world, alter it.

For years you are gone. Then one Monday, when I am to meet the Bishop in the parlour of the whorehouse, you are there instead. You stand up when I enter the room. You are sheepish. And I think of the first time I saw you, so miserable with your fedora in your hands between your knees. We stand there, regarding one another. I am pleased that I still have some power over you. My face is expressionless.

"Some sherry?"

"Yes, please," you say.

I cross the room to the cupboard.

I feel nothing, and yet my hand trembles as I lift the crystal stopper from the decanter.

I could turn and hurl it at you.

Instead, I carry two glasses and hand you one.

I sit down.

I watch your face and wait.

You say I'm looking well. A lie. I have lost weight and my nerves are frayed. I am, as you English say, "bearing up well under the strain." A strain, I realize, you know nothing about.

"Thank you."

I nod, without taking my eyes from your face.

"I understand you have an apartment in Faubourg."

"I still see clients here at the house."

"Have you a phone?"

"Yes."

"Good. That will make things easier."

I have no idea what you mean by "things."

"Well, then," you say, draining your glass and rising.

"Of course," I say, setting my glass down and leading you upstairs.

The awkwardness continues once we're in the room. You fumble with the many buttons of my silk blouse, a particular favourite of the Bishop's precisely because of the number of buttons.

I brush your hands away, turn, and finish undressing myself.

Then I hand you a flogger.

You give me a quizzical look.

"Use it," I say and turn my back to you.

Nothing happens. I grab it from your hand and sweep it across the bed.

"Doucement au début. Comme chatouiller. Ensuite plus dur. Comme ça. Je te dirigerai."

I turn away and wait again.

You begin by laying the flogger over my back like a drape. You drag it softly.

"Bien. Oui, comme ça."

You lift it and let the tips of its leather ribbons graze my flesh.

Your first strike is just right. Not too sharp, well placed over the shoulder blade. And your rhythm is perfect.

You stop and cover my back with soft kisses. Then begin again.

Slowly with steady, even strokes. Tentative at first, then with more assurance.

"Plus fort."

You stop, then start again in earnest.

It stings.

Finally, I can feel again.

You are excited. On fire. We clutch one another, tumble onto the bed, and you come into me savagely, tenderly, knowing, somehow, what you will never understand.

For the first time in weeks, I am fully alive.

October 1970. Not long after the Quebec Liberation Front executes one of its hostages, you come to see me.

Your hands shake. I notice how we have both aged.

You're so angry, you cannot speak.

Or scared.

When you are in states like these—and they are rare—I think you are breaking it off again. I prepare for your reasoned approach, how "seeing" me doesn't make sense. It's a curious expression of yours—"seeing" me. As if I were a spectre or a phantom, a dream you keep trying to wake from.

But you are shaking, so I reach out to hold your hands steady. "What is it?"

You pull your hands away. "There was a mailbox in the garden."

I nod. I wait, facing you, with my hands in my lap.

You ask me what it means. A warning? A death threat from the separatists who have been blowing up pillar boxes in Montreal?

How should I know what it means, this?

I feel pinned to the wall. Accused.

No matter how I answer, I am implicated because I am French—in the same way that you are to blame because you are English.

"What should we do?" you ask.

"What makes you think I would know?"

"You understand these people—how they think, how they work."

"And who are *these people*?"

We look at each other in silence. The room fills with pure rage, like snow.

You mean people like me because I am among the people about whom you know nothing. The shopkeepers and labourers of whom you take no notice. Now suddenly it makes "sense" to be "seeing" us.

Now there is a mailbox at the bottom of the rectory garden, and you want to know what it means. You come to me, a small half-brown woman who was not born here, a girl from the orphanage whom you met in a whorehouse, the Bishop's mistress and now yours, with whom you've grown into middle age … come to me because I'm supposed to understand—*these people*.

Because they are *my* people?

That's all you really know.

Now it is you who is pinned by the silence. Your insult shimmers all around us.

"Help me. Helen is beside herself. Are we in danger?"

If I were cruel, if I wanted to play with you, I could say, "These are dangerous times." But I shake my head. "I have no way of knowing, but I think you are safe."

What I don't say is that, in the end, you have no real power—as white, as English as you are, in the end you are insignificant. Which may well be a bigger insult. A middle-aged vicar in Sillery. Who would pay your ransom? Who would even know who you are?

I'm a bit flattered that you'd think that these young toughs would have anything to do with me, who, after all, is also insignificant—invisible. A forty-five-year-old woman with a string bag at the market. No, James. Here's what you fail to understand. They have more in common with a motorcycle gang than with ... someone like me. They are thugs, anti-intellectuals. They'd just as soon burn down the library as a bank, free Quebec of its books. What do they know of our poets? What do they care, so long as the fire burns brightly enough to make it onto the television evening news. *La libération du Québec*, indeed! We are all the same to them, anyone who is not whoever they think they are.

Which sets me to wondering who you think I am—after all these years.

For whatever reason, you disappear again, this time for good.

From now on, you show up only in my paintings—crude figures, verging on pornographic, a face of suffering, a face of beatific transcendence. You become a sort of icon. The process of painting these becomes an act of prayer. Remembering you through invention. In some ways the most abstract painting of all.

For what was your body?

How was it muscled? What was your posture?

It changed, of course, as you aged. You remained tall, though somewhat stooped. The hair on your chest became grey. The hair on your shins and your ankles wore away from socks. Your hands remained the hands of a priest, devoted to the sacraments, not the work of this world. You developed a paunch, but remained thin.

I remember your touch, your fire, the sound of your breath in my ear, the resonance of your voice.

I remember your desire, your shyness, and how you overcame it with such sudden ardour. And how you changed as you dressed in silence, gathered your clothes, and assembled yourself carefully to go back to the world you were in but not of.

Or was that your real world, in the end? That "other" life you lived when we were apart? The life of a cleric and a husband?

I have started to fall. On ice the first time; I landed on my backside, thought nothing of it.

The next time, it wasn't ice. I simply lost my footing.

It was curious—my feet going out from under me—not obeying, somehow. The physician knocked my knees and elbows with his rubber hammer. He shone a light into each eye, listened to my heart and found no complaint. He even sent me to a specialist who scanned my brain.

"Pas de problème," he said. *"Normal."*

And yet I keep falling.

No mystery, I suppose.

It is my age. I am seventy-four.

Toutes nos petites morts, our little deaths, and somehow I thought you would be here with me at the end. I kept imagining you at my bedside, holding my hand as I drifted in and out of consciousness. All these little deaths, these transports, the sweet recovery, the return to consciousness. Sometimes I thought we would go together, be found peacefully entwined in one another's arms, a challenge for the undertakers to separate. Ah! Mine at last. In death ... Beyond death. An idle fantasy.

I never imagined outliving you, James.

Your funeral was simple, dignified, performed by a colleague I seem to remember you disliked. I can't be sure. Helen seemed both shrunken and somehow triumphant. I gave my condolences to her at the end. Her eyes shone through the thin black veil, and I thought of my father's people in the desert. I clasped her white-gloved hand and said, "I'm sorry."

She smiled and thanked me.

"Your friendship meant so much to James."

I wanted to take her in my arms and rock her. I imagined I could hear her keening and could imagine her lunging for me, trying to claw my eyes out for the hours I'd stolen from her. But no. She was not merely civil, she was kind. Genuinely so. And it took courage for her to acknowledge me at all.

What had we lost, your wife and I?

Your touch. Your dry cough when you were nervous and wanted to change the subject. Your smooth cock with its perfect mushroom head. The wiry grey hair over your breastbone. The smooth hair of your forearms. Your perfectly pared nails, the deep lines of your knuckles in repose. The loose skin of your broad back. The smell of your neck. Your arms. Your arms. Your long feet. The sweet look of utter bewilderment on your face when I tried to describe what was important to me. How I gave up trying as my life became too complicated, too dangerous to let you know about.

They say you died at home with Helen at your side, nursing your flu, while the vestry committee waited downstairs.

I see your handsome profile against the smooth white pillow, the glare behind the window shade. I can almost feel your head throb. What were your thoughts, James? Did you call for me? And if you had, would Helen have sent for me? Perhaps.

I see the tumbler on your bedside table, the glass smudged with grey and a spoon stuck in it. Pill bottles. Tissues. No book. You are too ill to read, even. You are exhausted, ready to leave us, having made some prior agreement with God not to grow dotty and forgetful and nod off to sleep, mistaking it for prayer.

"Holy Mary, Mother of God, pray for us sinners now and in the hour of our death."

Not the prayer on your lips.

The prayer always on mine.

You slip away without Helen noticing at first. Perhaps she is reading the psalms or knitting. She imagines you returning to good health. She has no idea of your decision to leave us. Ever considerate, you slip away without gasping or clutching. There is perhaps one rattle, a cough, and then you are gone.

Helen looks up. She may even be about to say, "Yes, dear?" And at first she does not know you've slipped out of her reach forever. It takes a moment, and then she is filled with real panic that will, in the coming weeks, turn to rage, none of which she will show.

We stand a long moment gazing at one another, her eyes shining behind the veil. We do not let our clasped hands go, and I notice a reptilian coolness inside the glove.

Of course. She is not there. She has tried to follow you beyond. Beyond. And in some impossible way we seem to know that we will go on sharing you, and there is the sudden shiver of your presence in our bones.

I let go of Helen's hand, bow slightly, resist one last urge to put my hands on her shoulders and kiss her once on each cheek through the veil. I make my way across the narthex and out the door. I cross the street and carefully tread the icy gravel paths of the cemetery where you will be buried.

Over a thin crust of snow, I walk through the gravestones to where I can see the river.

From my table in the café, I can see the mirror and the street through the window, two worlds forever flowing into each other then separating again. The angle is such that I can watch without being seen.

The people through the window appear suddenly at the edge of the mirror, the same edge into which the others, walking in the opposite direction, disappear.

When I leave, I walk out of the mirror, pass through the door, into the street. I don't want to go back to the studio and I'm not ready to go home, so I go on walking, *à la dérive*, without purpose or intent.

The Bishop

Flagstaff, Maine, where I was born, is underwater now. Sometimes I dream that I return—swimming—and that it's all as it must have been, only flooded—everything wavering, as it does when reflected, but murky with river-bottom silt. It's not deep. Nowhere is the lake the power company made very deep—so I imagine the tops of the church steeples breaking the surface, with a buoy to alert pleasure boaters. In fact the town was abandoned, dismantled, and then submerged in 1950 when they built the hydroelectric dam. But when I return in dreams, it is intact, underwater.

My mother said there was an earthquake on the night I was born. As my head appeared, the light above her began to swing in a circle. She took it as a sign. She could feel the earth tremble as she pushed and pain rocked her body. She

said her waters rose to fill the fissure opened by the earthquake, and the town was inundated. Though she died long
before the hydroelectric dam, she somehow knew the fate
of her village.

How my mother made it back to Flagstaff with a brown
baby in her belly, or how she made it to wherever she met
my father, or how and where they met, or how he found
her again is still a mystery. My mother would get a dreamy
look in her eye and tell a tale that might include a dwarf or
a flying canoe.

Whatever led up to it, I know for certain that I was born
on September 1, 1925, in rooms my grandmother rented
above the general store—at least that's how the story goes.
I'm not sure what happened to the birth certificate. They
say my father arrived at some point—out of nowhere. Out
of a cloud of blowing snow, this brown man came walking
in the middle of winter. I remember a dusky smell, and a
deep melodious, cooing voice that may have been my father's. And his touch. Being lifted and lifted higher and then
swung around—which my mother says I loved, and which
stopped when he died.

For, the next summer, he was eaten by a threshing
machine.

Or not.

There may have been no sudden arrival, no tragic end
in the threshing machine. What I imagine I remember of
my father is just that—what I imagine. How my mother got
from Maine to Paris (where she says she met my father) and
back is a mystery. In one story, she joins a carnival in August
and travels with them to the sea, where she boards a tramp
steamer to Africa and is taken to a tribe where she becomes
a favourite of the king, who later sends her to France for
reasons that are not clear, but there she is in Paris, and down

on her luck, and she falls in with artists and anarchists, and among them meets the man who would become my father.

Father—that most abstract of nouns.

The rest of my "history" is my memory, which, given circumstances and my mother's tales, is exaggerated, if not entirely made up. Did I invent the Second World War? Could I claim to have experienced it when I did not live under the Gestapo? Did it, in fact, occur in Canada? If it happened in my imagination, isn't it true that it happened? And if so, how? And if not, how not? Once I had surrendered myself wholly to dream and intuition, were they not "reality" for me? So it is all true: the red dress, the brown man, the threshing machine, the flood—and the flying canoe my mother took to Europe and then back again to Maine.

In dreams, I see my mother's town intact, rotting slowly, underwater—the church, its steeple, the schoolhouse, desks, kitchen chairs, linens with their slow, underwater movement, as if blown by some viscous wind. Nothing floats to the surface. Boats glide over the town. Light insists itself through the murky green and spreads into gradual refraction from a broken windowpane. Beds float through doors. Chairs, hammers, nails, and dishes float sideways, never to the surface. A slow mobile world that stays in close proximity to itself.

The Germans invaded Poland on my fourteenth birthday. September 1, 1939. It was the sign I'd been waiting for. I'd been at the orphanage of the Sisters of the Good Shepherd since coming to Quebec City with my mother as a small child, and it was time to flee. I'd been planning in ways even secret to myself for some time. There was a fluttering in me, a stirring in the world—a quickening. I read the signs, watched for omens, the Great War in the Heavens reflected here on earth. But it was not as the priests supposed. It was something far greater and far smaller reflected in our own hearts. The veils grew thin. What was unseen became visible to me.

In the dream, I am in bed between two criminals, men who've slipped into the convent. We are trying to sleep. I lie on my right side; one of the men is in back of me, the other in front. I try not to let them feel my desire, but they know.

In the dream, I rise for rounds in the morning and walk the corridors of the dormitory. On the ground floor, I encounter people dressed, ready to flee. They are intent but not frightened. Once the door is opened, I notice it is snowing.

Never have I been so glad to see snow. The silence. The stillness. I feel I can move from one enclosed house to another without being detected in the world, as if I can walk on top of the snow without leaving a print. I'm not yet ready. Not yet of age. If I were caught, I would be brought back, punished, sent to somewhere I couldn't get away from.

In the dream, I know where to go, and once I slip away from the convent, I follow first one street and then another, recognizing what I've never before seen in waking life.

Weeks later, I manage my actual escape from the orphanage. I wake before the others. It is still dark. I gather a few things, what I've gathered in my mind hundreds of times before, and walk calmly, quietly through the dormitory and down the stairs, through the refectory, the kitchen, and out the door. I walk for hours, ducking into alleys to avoid the police, anyone, until long after daybreak. Then I remember the dream streets and circle back to find them. I follow them slowly, deliberately, one after another, standing still from time to time to close my eyes and wait for the next picture.

I hear voices. I come across a tall thin house in a courtyard. Women are outside doing the washing. Singing. That's what I'm drawn to, a song that is quick and lively, yet mournful. One woman's voice and then the others join in on the chorus. I stand at the entranceway to the courtyard and listen, transfixed. I have never heard anything so beautiful. Deep and resonant, so unlike the thin, reedy voices of the nuns. One of the women sees me and motions me forward instead of shooing me away. It's strange, looking back. The courtyard, the house itself, the women singing, and strangest of all, this motion forward. The steps I take in the next moment will change my life forever.

"*Tu t'es perdue?*" asks one of the women.

I shake my head, no.

"Do you know where you are?" she asks, turning back to the house.

I say no.

"Well then, you are lost, aren't you?"

"No," I say.

And all the women laugh.

"Come here," she says. "How did you find us?"

I decide not to lie. "I kept having dreams. I'm trying to remember the way that was shown to me in the dreams."

"But where do you come from?"

I step back, afraid that if I tell them, they'll make me return.

"She's an orphan," says one of the other women.

I turn to run away, but the first woman calls me back.

"Don't worry. You're not in trouble. Come here. Are you looking for work?"

"Arienne, don't. She's just a kid."

"We need a housekeeper. How old are you?"

"Seventeen," I say.

"Maybe fifteen and a half. I'd say closer to thirteen," says Arienne. "Am I right?"

"Fourteen," I say, "but I'm not a child."

"I can see that," she says, smiling. "Do you know who we are? What we do?"

"I heard the singing; it was so beautiful, I thought you must be angels."

They bend over, slap one another on the back. One laughs so hard, she starts to cough.

Arienne smiles.

"*Nous sommes des prostituées. Ici c'est une maison mal famée.* Do you understand?"

I nod, though I do not really understand much at all. Except that this very spot on earth is what the sisters had tried to save me from, a place I now feel destiny has led me to. I'm full of conflicting emotions. I know how my mother died; I know something about how she lived. It's not what I am destined to become, but it's nothing to fear, either. I sense this is the place I've been looking for. I wonder what might happen if I'm wrong.

I pause to consider if I feel any danger, and I do not, so I let Arienne show me my small room off the kitchen. And soon we sit down to a lunch of sausage, potatoes, and roasted apples.

How it began is how it continued pretty much throughout the war. That first meal together set the tone: bragging, tall tales, unbridled hilarity, merciless teasing—more love than I think I had ever encountered in my life. I mean from so many all at once. A family, not without its troubles, but a sense of loyalty and belonging that I later found out was the envy of other women in what became my trade.

So I started out in the kitchen, chopping, peeling, pre-paring soups, baking. I'd rise early and make my own coffee with bread and jam. I usually had quite a bit of time, since no one stirred much before ten o'clock. I'd clean the parlour, dust the books and crystal goblets, the lamps. I'd tidy the entrance hall. I'd be sure to have coffee ready and bread sliced and a pot of jam on the table once the girls began to emerge for breakfast. I wasn't allowed upstairs at first. I think Arienne didn't want to scare me off, and she wanted to be sure she could trust me, so she waited to initiate me to the mysteries gradually.

We fell into a rhythm. Mondays the house was closed to all but the Bishop and his guests. Everyone treated me well, with the exception of Beata, who seemed jealous of me. She'd been the youngest until I came. The others liked me and protected me. Their teasing became part of my education.

And Beata became what was called in the convent "a particular friend." I saw the need to win her over. I knew I could not afford an enemy—anywhere. We were often assigned housework chores together, which she resented because she had already begun to see clients and felt herself to be more privileged than I. As a convent orphan, I knew a thing or two about hierarchy, and accepted her authority—or rather did nothing to challenge it, small as it was, which is not the same thing as accepting it, I suppose.

I came to like her quite a lot. She was straightforward, with a sweetness and vulnerability that showed themselves as she came to trust me more. Little by little, we became friends, combing out one another's hair, sometimes sleeping in the same bed, which led to petting and kissing—giving pleasure, reassurance, comfort. Embraces and even sex— desire without the heat of ownership. Maybe that was the difference between our friendship and our relations with men. We had the fierce protectiveness of sisters as well as a playful tenderness and a secret language of gesture and glance. Small jokes about the clients and the other girls.

Now the orphanage is a museum. There are photographs

from before the time I was there. In one, three young women are graduating. It is 1905. A crown of flowers, each girl holding a bouquet in one hand, a rolled-up diploma in the other. Smiling.

I borrow the girl in the middle, the one who looks happiest, most confident. She becomes my mother in the story I invent, so that my mind comes from somewhere I can point to. Here. My mother went to school, got a diploma.

In truth, my mother was barely literate—in either language. When she did go to school, the nuns humiliated her in what they claimed was Parisian French. Of course the sisters had no more seen Paris than we had, but that, they insisted, was the language they spoke. My mother was so quiet, they thought she was deaf. She simply refused to speak, so people would leave her alone. The moment she realized that men would pay to empty themselves into her body, she disappeared for three years and reappeared in a torn red silk dress with me in her belly.

By then, she had learned to speak Parisian French.

I remember my mother holding my hand on the ferry and my first sight of Quebec, the city on the hill, our mutual excitement and silent terror. My father dead. My mother fleeing north across the border for obscure reasons, more than half crazy with grief. I am no more than five years old. It is the Great Depression. Poverty. The oldest story in the world, so my mother embarked once again into the oldest profession in the world as a solution. She died some years later of syphilis, but not before she was arrested and turned over to the Sisters of the Good Shepherd, where we were separated for my own good. I was too big for the white iron crib they put me in, and I remember trying to make myself smaller and smaller, so I could start the story over again, get born anew in a farm house, the air full of birdsong. A real family with a mother and father and *pépés* and *mémés* who were delighted to see me instead of ashamed. It was bad enough to be a bastard, but a brown bastard.

And French spoken freely.

Our French, not theirs.

How quickly the city I thought would save us turned into a prison.

I think of how it shone so, the city I saw from the ferry. It might as well have been Jerusalem. I could see right through to the radiant heart of it.

We did not live, at first, in the radiant heart of Quebec, though we were excited (I thought). For my mother, as I look back, I know it must have been terror, that frenzy of back alleys. Sailors. Stairways. Men dressed as women. The smell of damp wool. Wind. Puddles I had to jump over. A red door. Scullery maids turned out of their jobs, wandering drunk. A haunted kind of rough laughter full of what I now recognize as despair.

I remember the late afternoon sunlight. Bare trees. The yellow brick of a Jesuit dormitory. A man with a knife. Screams. Fighting. Someone grabbed my hand, picked me up suddenly, whisked me away. How could I not have found it exciting? I was exotic, a brown doll people fawned over, making my mother's life both easier and more difficult.

I survived.

She didn't.

It's as simple as that.

I like to remember that first vision of Quebec City from the south shore. It took my breath away. I loved it and would love and hate it from that day on. I seemed to sense my whole future and accept the challenge willingly, at five, the autumn of 1930. A walled city, a fortress to protect—protect what?

Who? Me? My mother? The priests? The lumber barons? Against whom? The Indians? The English? The Irish scullery maids in Basse-Ville at the bottom of the hill?

I loved school in the orphanage. The desks, the chalk-board, the pens, the ink, even the musty smell of it. I was voracious—overeager, even impudent—in my desire to learn. I frightened some of the nuns, inspired others. I played the emotions of each one, separately, without any aim other than knowing more, reading more. I made myself irresistible. I felt I was dedicating my life to God, and so I was. But my vocation was clearly never as a *religieuse.* I knew that early on. And I don't think I purposefully misled the sisters. I couldn't have possibly explained what I meant by vocation.

I had no words for it then.

And now? What are the words for it now?

If God had not meant me to be the Anglican Bishop's mistress, the Lord would have found somebody else, but I was perfect for the job: a girl from the convent, an orphan. My English was better than most. I was lively, intelligent, well-read. An artist into the bargain. I could be mistress, daughter, and precocious student all in one.

I did not begin as the Bishop's mistress of course. I began as a housekeeper, under the fierce protection of Arienne. When the Bishop expressed interest in me, he went through her, and when she broached the subject with me, she was delicate.

"But Arienne," I said, "I am not a virgin."

I told her about the dance, the ill-fitting dresses donated by the parish women, walking in a neat line, and the drunk who stumbled against me, drew back, and spat a long line of brown across my dress. I stood still, mortified, and one of the sisters grabbed my hand and walked me back to the orphanage. There was no other dress to wear but my uniform, so I changed, and Sister and I hurried to meet the others at the dance. Curiosity and excitement outweighed my shame, and the minute I entered the room I was spellbound by the lights, the girls and boys dressed in makeshift formal clothes, the accordion, the man calling the dances. Even the sisters looked merry and lighthearted. What was this magic? I wondered. And where had it been all my life?

Soon enough, a boy invited me to dance.

It took some time to arrange the rendezvous, and it was both more and less than anything I could have imagined. Still, I was full of hope that somehow he or this would carry me further, carry me away. What I remember is a crumpled-up dollar bill on the bed when I turned around, buttoning my blouse after it was over. He didn't look at me. At first I didn't know what to think. I wondered where he had found this small fortune in the years of the Great Depression. Perhaps he had dropped it by mistake. I picked it up to give it back to him, but he shooed me away and continued out the door.

I was offended. But then, I was suddenly rich. I had found the means of escape. I was ashamed and elated all at once. It happened that fast, in an instant. I snuck back into the orphanage, which was easy enough, but where to hide this treasure? How to hide my new power from the nuns—for if there is one thing they hate, it is the power they feel they lack—and how was I to use these new gifts in the world?

This is what I contemplate in chapel in the weeks that follow. What I dream about in geography class. The question I pose to God when I pray. I live among my classmates like a ghost. I have silent allies who will cover for me if I am ever missed. But I am never missed. I am judicious, scrupulous, careful to show my submissiveness to the sisters, even my love. For I am free to love them now more fully. Having had my first man, of course, I now pity the sisters. My pride is of a different sort, one I must conserve like a magical skill to use in the world where I am bound. This is what sets me apart: some of my schoolmates will end up as two-bit whores, whereas I shall become mistress to the Anglican Bishop.

Not all at once.

Gradually. By degrees.

When the time comes, I am bathed and dressed by Arienne and reminded of my manners. I practise my curtsy. She is proud and stern and excited for me, like a mother preparing her daughter for a suitor. Nostalgic in some way, perhaps. Not envious.

Arienne is incapable of envy.

I am led into the parlour where he sits in his red plush throne, with a glass of sherry on the table beside him. I notice the light in the cut glass, the whitish lines across the amber. I am lost, looking at what the light does, until Arienne speaks.

"Thérèse, this is the Bishop."

He rises and extends his hand.

I take it but do not kiss his ring. I am Catholic. He is Anglican. I bend to my deepest curtsy.

"*Monseigneur.*"

"*Enchanté,*" he responds, smiling down at me.

I rise slowly, meeting his gaze, and he beckons me to take the seat next to him.

He asks if I'd care to join him in a glass of sherry.

Arienne shakes her head.

"I see," says the Bishop. "Well then, tell me what you know."

I am cautious, as if it were an examination, which it is, in a sense. I begin with the succession of the English monarchy, the Magna Carta, the triumphs of Elizabeth the First.

He is amused. Emboldened, I recite a Shakespeare sonnet. He is astonished. When I profess my love for Wordsworth, he is smitten.

Soon he has me reading forbidden books. Balzac, Zola, George Sand. I struggle with Voltaire. I have no real concept of irony. Much of his satire is lost on me, and I object to his cynicism. We move on then. I come to love Victor Hugo, and then there is Flaubert, who for a time is my favourite. I read the books in French. We discuss them in English when the Bishop's French fails him. In the bedroom, however, he forbids me to speak English. It is always in French that we make love—and not the French of literature, but the *joual* of the street that excites him no end.

He calls me Odalisque, after the Turkish slave in the paintings. Odalisque is who I become to myself. It is Odalisque who has courage or grace or discretion—whatever quality is called for that I feel I lack at the moment. It is Odalisque who is compelled to record her thoughts in these notebooks.

Arienne is shocked by the books I read, though she cannot read herself and is not by any means a prude. She knows they are on the Church's list of banned books. She fears *la loi du cadenas*, the Padlock Law, which could close the house and put us all in jail. It's one thing to be a prostitute (under the full protection—one might even say the blessing—of the Anglican Bishop). It's quite another to be accused of entertaining dangerous ideas, all of which are now called *communiste*. There, she fears, the Bishop's power might not protect us. No one is more powerful than Duplessis and his Union Nationale, even though he is no longer Premier. It's hard to tell what Arienne fears most: Duplessis or the Liberal government we have between his terms. I learn not to talk to Arienne about these ideas; they don't interest her anyway. And so for years it is only to the Bishop that I may speak my full mind.

Almost.

My first time with the Bishop, I notice his belly, how smooth it is. I am already in the room, in a white dressing gown, rather frilly, rather formal. I am propped up on pillows, as if I were ill. There's a knock on the door. I've been instructed not to rise to answer it but to call from the bed: *"C'est qui?"*

He answers and requests to be admitted.

"Entrez, s'il vous plaît, Monseigneur."

He opens the door slowly and steps into the room, bowing. He holds flowers and a box of chocolates, as if he were a schoolboy. He is scrubbed pink and merry about the eyes, like St. Nicholas. He is beside himself with anticipation, and for a moment I'm worried. How can I possibly live up to this? Then I remember. It is for this the Bishop has come: to instruct me.

He extends his hand, so I extend my own, and he guides me to a small table that has been covered with a new cloth. There comes another knock on the door. It's Arienne, this time with a decanter of sherry and two small crystal glasses on a silver tray. Without looking at me, she sets the tray down on the table, and I'm given to understand that it's all right for me to join the Bishop in a glass. She bows and smiles to the Bishop, says if there is anything else he wishes, to simply ring the bell, a satin rope that hangs by the headboard and sounds in the kitchen, and it is only before she turns to leave the room that she meets my gaze and smiles at me with such radiance I am breathless. Looking back, I remember it as perhaps the most poignant blessing of my life.

Then it is just the Bishop and me and two glasses of sherry and small talk with shy silences between. As his cheeks become rosier, the Bishop begins to compliment my beauty, my eyes, my hands, my pale loveliness. I burst out laughing. I can't help myself. I am not pale, I am brown, a mulatto. The Bishop looks sheepish and then laughs with me. The conventions of English poetry can only go so far. And yet it is what we both love, and so the Bishop recites "My mistress' eyes are nothing like the sun" and I love him for this.

He takes my hand, smiles, expresses his appreciation for my friendship, and then leads me to the high bed. I stand before it and he begins to loosen my dressing gown. I notice first his pudgy fingers, the humility of their hesitations, their *listening*, you might say, and then his eyes, gazing into mine, questioning, waiting for my permission. The exquisitely slow pace, so different from that boy those many months ago in the furtive room. Here we have all the time in the world, and I am called upon to say yes, like the Blessed Virgin.

And the gown slips off my shoulders.

Our house was hidden from the street. You wouldn't have known to look for it through *la ruelle*, which opened into a small courtyard. It was like a country house with a stone foundation, but narrow, too tall for itself. Crooked. Drunk. The Bishop called it *le bateau ivre*. It was painted battleship grey—what else during the war?—with paint stolen for us by the sailors. Then after the war we managed to get reds and pale blues and yellows. Someone painted on architectural details. The house, inside and out, became a *trompe l'oeil*, which it always was, even painted grey. I mean in spirit. Each room was a different world. The formal parlour might as well have been a vicarage. Red plush, mauves, purples. Brocades and satin and silk. Leather-bound books along one wall and crystal lamps and goblets. A Persian carpet on the floor. Surrounded by ordinary tenements, the house was all the more curious. Dark and cool in the summer, a world submerged in dreaming. Warm with firelight and lamplight in winter.

Magical.

Ideal for the arts practised there.

Washing day, Monday of course, we hoist the linens, silks, dressing gowns like flags along lines connected to the roofs of surrounding buildings. With the laundry out, in the wind, the house looks as if it might lift off the earth. Sometimes I still think of it rising to set sail across the moon.

Le bateau ivre, indeed.

A drunken boat. A house of dreams, parallel lives, secret pleasures, exquisite agonies.

So much joy and good humour in those hard times.

Mondays in good weather, we haul the washtubs into the yard, and one of us, Bridgett usually, starts to sing. A folk song, something good to work by, with a regular rhythm and lots of verses, as we scrub the sheets on the boards and put bluing on them and string some on lines from posts in the yard, and then hang the others out the fourth-storey window or off the roof. The house becomes a tall-masted schooner. Bodices, bustiers, brassieres billowing in the updrafts, high enough to where some sun might reach them. And below we scrub and sing of false love, delusion, broken hearts, and open graves. Or the heroism of peasant soldiers in popular revolt. We are always closed on Monday. We scour the place top to bottom. Only the Bishop and his special guests are allowed to call on Monday evenings.

Other evenings at the house, over an early supper, we discuss the topics of the day.

"Vote?" cries one of the older women. "Why would I want to vote? Look who I'd have to vote *for*!"

"Idiots. Like all men," says Natalie.

"But what about *le bonhomme* Godbout, who offers free primary school for the kids? He's not so bad."

"Now that we have the vote," I say, "we must use it. Otherwise nothing will change."

"My dad lost his arm—up to the elbow!—in an accident at his factory just last year."

"And what about wages?"

"You're talking like communists. Let God's will work through Premier Duplessis."

"The will of God! You make me laugh! How can that jackass do the will of God? Besides, he's the Premier, not the Pope."

"Don't tell *him* that!"

"It's not a woman's place—politics."

"And exactly what is a woman's place?" cries Natalie.

"Right here in the *bordel*, where we belong. A fair wage. Three meals a day. All the right men for company. And no diapers!"

Everyone laughs.

"Yes, but what about women in the factories?" I cry. "Women in the army? We can't improve their conditions without strong labour unions."

Beata nods, though she'd prefer not to take any stand at all. I'm her best friend, and she doesn't want me to be alone.

"You read too much, Thérèse. It's making you old before your time."

"Look what happened in the asbestos mines."

Arienne slaps her palm on the table and calls a halt to the discussion.

"*Ça y est! J'en ai marre!*" she says. "The Padlock Law is still in effect no matter what the Liberals say. The police can come at any time and search us for no reason at all. The truth is, we are not free, and we must be careful. The police could close us down, and we could all end up in jail. I suggest we change the subject. And there'll be no joining the picket lines, Thérèse. Understood?"

Le comédien visits the house on Tuesdays at 2:00 p.m. That's his regular time. He is tall and lean and very proud. Handsome, strong, *comme il faut*. And worried all the time about his looks, the part he has in a current play. Or getting a new part. He complains about the director, his leading lady.

He worries that he's growing fat.

It is with him, lying under him, waiting for him to reach his *petite mort*, that I realize if they come for me now, if they burst through the door with their pistols drawn, if they set fire to the house, I would die in the arms of a man I didn't love. And so I decide to love them all as Christ loves them, as Mary loves them, as if—and who's to know that it's not true—each one were the Beloved Himself, the Guest sent to test my loving, the last chance, the last moment in which to live my faith. And so I vow to love each one as the last man on earth, an emblem of all men.

One day, after he leaves, I sit with my book, trying to describe this—buzzing—a rhythm in my own blood—but what is it?—the fire around us?—the burning to ashes and rising again?

An ascent in a column of light, a current that sweeps us up into God only knows.

What I'm willing to suffer in order to be transformed.

There's a soft knock on the door. Someone needs the room, and here I sit writing.

"*Un moment,*" I say.

"Are you all right?" asks the voice from the other side of the door.

"*Oui, oui,*" I say. "*Ça va. Ça va. J'arrive!*"

I pull the sheets from the bed, remake it, sprinkle drops of rosewater on the fresh pillowcases, replace the duvet. I throw on my robe, grab my dress, and head for the bath, my book under my arm.

She's not annoyed, Beata. Not really. She knows the state I'm in. Sometimes I think of the nuns in Avila holding St. Teresa down to keep her from one of her ascensions. It's only that others wait—only because we're so busy.

As I pass, Arienne eyes me as if she's worried. She often has that look these days. She says I've taken on too much work here at the house and modelling at the École des beaux-arts. She's concerned on my behalf, but also for the Bishop and his pleasure. He is, after all, our patron and my benefactor. My primary responsibility is to him. And so I mustn't exhaust myself with all the rest of it. All this she says in one glance. And I try in my return look to reassure her that I've understood.

My life after the war becomes more complex. I continue to live at the *bateau ivre*, but my spirit expands outside the house. I meet Theo, a student at the École des beaux-arts, after I start modelling privately for another student and then as one of the regular models. The Bishop overrides Arienne's initial objections. He argues that it will do me good, broaden my horizons, and explains we are indeed living in a new world. It is Theo who one day puts a paintbrush in my hand, takes my shoulders, turns me toward an empty canvas, and cries, "Begin!" And so I make the first gestures that will once again change my life.

The Bishop rents an apartment for me to use as a studio. Theo and his chum Renard often visit, and then end up living there. My life and work at the house continue, but I have a life outside. I want for nothing. What I need has a habit of appearing, as if by magic.

In my twenties, I feel quite seasoned and worldly-wise. Yet I am aware of the delicacy of my position with Arienne and the girls, as well as with the Bishop: discretion is of the utmost. I inhabit two worlds, several different worlds. I have many roles, each one of which I play with increasing skill and ease. In this I've been well trained by Arienne.

And yet I must tread carefully. There are dangers of which I am only half-aware. I must not abuse or flaunt my privilege.

The summerhouse has a stove. That's the first thing I notice as Mister Z opens the door for me. I step in. After the stove, I notice a woman kneeling beside the door, dressed in an ornate kimono and wearing an elaborate hairstyle (I later learn it is a wig) with sticks and strings of pearls. Her face is painted as if for the stage. I am repulsed and fascinated. I have never seen anything quite like it before. She pours us tea unlike anything I have ever tasted. Weak, vaguely sweet, green. The music of strange stringed instruments is playing on the phonograph. The walls are hung with silk tapestries—flowers, mountains, birds on thin branches floating in space.

I sit on the pillow beside Mister Z and am served tea by this ghost, this painted clown who says nothing. I know this is a test. I know not to reveal my ignorance. I know not to ask for sugar, even if it weren't rationed. I follow Mister Z's lead, and the lead of this strange actress who kneels before us and pours tea. And yet I look around, take it all in. I think: so this is where the English live. We have passed the large houses with lawns, turned into one of the long drives, and come around to this little place in the trees with a sparse garden.

The smiling clown woman invites me to my feet and beckons me behind a painted screen. Mister Z nods. Once there, she helps me to undress and then holds out the most astonishing robe I have ever seen: purplish black along the hem, rising into a thin blush of mauve, then white to the shoulder with a blossoming branch and a long-necked seabird. I find the material surprisingly light once she has pulled it onto my shoulders. And the sensation! Silk. Like water. She leads me back around the screen to present me to Mister Z, who smiles in approval. Then she disappears. I turn and she's gone. Where? I had thought there was only one door. Then I notice a drape, which must lead to another room. A small kitchen, perhaps.

Mister Z shows me the woodcuts he has promised— Japanese and Chinese prints of men and women making love. He points to one. I nod and smile—already I am becoming like the painted disappearing woman. I hold my head as if it had hair piled on top. I sit more erect. I open the robe to Mister Z's gaze and touch. He proceeds with such gradual curiosity that I'm the one who becomes impatient. How unlike the other men he is in this. And I am uncomfortable—hungry—which is exactly what he wants.

He opens the robe he has put on in my brief absence, and I see he is well pleased. He motions me to sit on him in the way we have seen in the prints, which is awkward at first. I shudder and cry out a little, mounting him, not because it hurts, but because I am surprised at the sensation. We sit like that for a long time, moving very little, while he instructs me in breath, which I think is absurd and find distracting, but I do it nonetheless. I am bored and uncomfortable. Mister Z seems to understand. We take breaks. I remember what I know from modelling about relaxing my body. He holds my back. He's much stronger than I have noticed before. Out of boredom, perhaps, I contract my vulva around his cock, and he gasps in delight, so I quicken the motion, then slow it down. At last, I have found something to do besides sit there. The pace is so slow, I do not yet know how to sense what is actually happening.

What feels like hours later, Mister Z takes me back to town.

This goes on for some months. He fetches me in his car, drives me to this house, and we have tea poured by the white-faced woman, who disappears. Then Mister Z and I sit in one of any number of positions for long periods of time, until he rings a bell and the geisha comes back to dress me. We drink more tea and then he returns me to the *bateau ivre*.

The other girls are curious and want to know all about it. No one is jealous. They are fascinated, but I find that I can say very little. When I describe what happens, they ask if that's all. And what do you feel, they ask. "Bored, sometimes. Curious, sleepy, uhmmm," and then I smile. Later I feel as if I am on fire, and the men I see after that give me extraordinary tips.

The Bishop makes discreet inquiries, which I dodge. Professional ethics. Confidentiality. Which he respects, but I can tell he is curious about how I am learning what I am learning. The other girls, I say. Whatever it is, he says, he is delighted, for himself and for the business. We are flourishing in those hard, hard times, when others suffer so. Each week at Mass, I put extra money in the poor box.

When I mount Mister Z in one of these sessions, I sit and am still, clenching my vulva and breathing, until I begin to feel his heat rising in me, the white light of his penetration in my spine, and on this day it reaches the top of my head— oh—slowly, slowly, and the tears at the corners of my eyes have the viscosity of sperm.

I am so raw after these sessions, which sometimes last for days, that I cannot be touched. In these times, I withdraw from the world and paint.

I simply reach for colours, mixing them, which soothes me. I spend forty minutes just mixing paint before I ever put brush to canvas. Without thinking. Instinct is what I paint from. And feeling.

Paint under my fingernails, and I've never seen Arienne so angry.

"What's this?"

"Oh. Paint. I was in the studio."

"Get it off—now. You can't see clients like this."

I go to the kitchen and find something under the sink that will take it off.

I know what she means—my hands, my touch. The men will notice the roughness.

Without intending to, I have crossed a line, violated an unspoken code of conduct. As carefully as I have tried not to, I have somehow flaunted my privilege. My freedom, my life outside the house, puts everything in danger.

The Bishop continues to encourage and support me, asks what I am painting.

"Oh, nothing really. Just studies. Flowers, mostly. *Les natures mortes.*"

But then I begin to suspect the Bishop and Arienne of talking behind my back, colluding. The mounting tension in the house signals the beginning of the end for me. I am sometimes late, often distracted. I wonder if the patrons don't talk about it among themselves and with the other girls. For the first time, I feel bad, not for being a whore, but for painting—and writing—and now even more than before, for the books that I read, or that I read books at all.

I get the sense, not from the Bishop but from Arienne, that my education is finished. Or ought to be. And it spreads to the other girls. Subtly I am left out of things, ostracized. Jealousies long dormant or set aside make themselves known—a scornful glance while passing in the corridor, a critical tone at mealtimes. Nothing overt, but I am more and more aware of the undercurrent of discontent and judgment against me.

Only Beata remains unwaveringly true. It's a loyalty born of pure love and a certain ignorance of the world, and when she touches me, she touches me all the more tenderly because of it. I swoon in the presence of this innocence, this pure spirit.

The Bishop's plan for me is generous. He has been setting aside money for me since the beginning, through Arienne, and it is this that Arienne says she wants to discuss with me one Monday morning in 1949 in the front parlour—alone.

"Thérèse, there is more than enough money now in your bank account. It is time you were out on your own. A young woman such as yourself, so bright … and … ambitious," she is quick to add. She cannot bring herself to look me in the eye.

"But this is my home," I protest.

"It can't be forever, my dear." And here she looks at me directly, and I can see she is near tears.

"Arienne, what is it?"

"We can't hold you here, Thérèse. You belong—I'm not sure how to say it—to something else, I think. Greater, perhaps. I've been selfish in keeping you here even this long."

That's it, I think, she's frightened. But when I look again into her eyes, I see it's not that simple. She wants something for me or for herself through me. She wants me to want something different, better, higher—something. She is acting out of a sense of duty, and she regrets the action.

"*Le Monseigneur* and I have decided"—she may as well

have said *your father and I have decided*—"that you would be better off…." And here she loses my attention.

She's a bad actress. I'm not convinced. And I am curiously indifferent to what they think is best for me. I'm angry. I don't want to be told what to do.

She knows she's taken the wrong tack. She begins again.

"Thérèse. It's time for you to leave home. It's as simple as that. If you don't like it after a few years, come back and we'll talk, but I couldn't live with myself…."

And there it is again, the false note. She has averted her gaze.

I move out of the house.

Quel départ!

Beata in tears, her arms around my neck. The bags packed. Awkward jokes. Arienne wishes me well, then turns away. And me? Confident, even aloof. I am leaving the only home I've ever really known. But I am determined to leave in style, in a *calèche*, in fact. (I'm on intimate terms with a number of drivers.)

My life will not change much. My centre of gravity is shifting, that's all. I'll be living in the apartment I share intermittently with Theo and Renard. I will still see the Bishop regularly at the house, will, in fact, still see some of my other regular patrons, and everyone lets me know I am welcome any time—on Mondays for the evening meal—or to help with the cleaning! An open invitation!

And they mean it. Suddenly the tension is gone.

Still, it is a melancholy moment, once the bags are in the *calèche*, and I hoist myself into the seat and turn to wave to the women gathered in the narrow passageway that leads into the *ruelle*.

"*Un moment!*" I call to the driver.

I leap back down and run toward them, sobbing. We hold each other for quite some time, until I break away and run to find Arienne sitting in her room with a glass of brandy.

She rises. We embrace. I take her face in my hands and cry, "*Je t'aime. Je t'aimerai toujours. Sans cesser! Pour l'éternité!*"

I run back downstairs, out the door, past my sisters, who part to let me through, and jump back into the *calèche*.

"Let's go," I cry. "*Vite! Vite!*"

Some weeks later, Beata comes to dinner at the apartment. She says she has a surprise, someone she wants me to meet, and in walks a tall, slender man in a poorly fitting suit, a felt hat in his right hand.

"This is Lionel," says Beata. I notice she is blushing. Her breathing is shallow, she is so excited.

"Lionel, this is Thérèse, my best friend," she continues.

I reach to shake his hand. He puts his hat back on his head; his left hand remains behind his back.

"I-I've heard so much about you," he stammers.

Beata and I burst into laughter, and now it is Lionel who blushes.

"Never mind," I say.

He produces the bouquet of wildflowers he has been hiding behind his back. I accept them with a deep bow.

I look over to Beata, as if to say: he is delightful. And to inquire about how serious this affair is. I know soon enough by watching—Beata will fill me in on everything later.

Except that she can't wait until later.

Over a little glass of whiskey, she tells the story of how they met at a dance in a union hall. I raise my eyebrows.

"Yes," she says. "I went despite Arienne's warnings. And it's not as if it were politics. It was a social event. And how else would I have met Lionel, here? It was fate, I tell you. Destiny."

She turns to smile at Lionel, who gazes into her eyes.

"When I saw her, I knew she was for me," says Lionel.

And he means it. I can tell. Whatever worry I have of his ability to protect Beata from the opinions of the world is dispelled by the way he touches her hand and gazes into her eyes. The flame of his simple ardour burns away any possible indecision or cowardice, and I see that he has it in him to face anything with Beata.

All this over *salade de tomates, une belle tourtière,* any number of bottles of beer.

It's not until I serve the coffee and the *tartes au sucre* that Beata mentions the stack of paintings in the corner.

"Oh!" says Beata, when I start pulling them out. Some are mine. Some are Theo's.

"Oh my! There they are!" she says. "So many colours! And all at once!"

"*Belles,*" says Lionel, nodding for emphasis, as if trying to convince himself. "*Très belles.*"

When the girls and I arrive at Beata's wedding, the fiddlers hold their bows suspended, one foot raised. The women putting out food stop and stare at us. We enter the court-yard together, wearing crimson, cobalt, and emerald-green satin gowns with large-brimmed hats and feather boas. We are shameless. We roll our hips, our chests thrust forward. We nod to those we pass in greeting. We are women from the other world come to send our sister into a respectable marriage. After a moment of stunned silence, a few of the rough younger men begin to applaud, and though they are properly scandalized, and however they may resent our presence, some of the elders join in making us feel welcome.

Like it or not, the bride has been one of us.

Beata cries out in delight, and then claps her hands again

and again, which begins a general round of applause. It's as if a circus has arrived, and some peer around us for the prancing horses and acrobats that are surely next to arrive, for everything is possible this day. So they laugh and applaud us as we encircle the bride and begin to sing *La Bastringue*, which the fiddlers take up, matching the increasingly rapid rhythm of our feet. Then we form a line, serpentine, gathering people one by one as we coil through the guests.

Le curé—Père Phillippe—looks quite terrified. We've had to do some convincing. More like blackmail. He is here to perform this wedding under duress because the child in Beata's belly might well be his—and he knows it. He is sweating in his black dress, the book clutched in his right hand. The old women think it's the heat; one brings him a glass of punch. But it's Divine Justice that makes him sweat today, not the sun. And we are here, in part, to make sure he does his job. I fix him in my gaze. His agony is transparent. He longs to join in, remembers what he knows of our bodies, aches to caress us. I stop short of drawing him into the dance; that would be too much. He is enduring torture enough.

He clears his throat, gestures to the musicians, briefly acknowledges the joy of the occasion, and calls us to order. Blackmail or no, he is doing what's right.

We encircle Beata again and walk her toward Lionel, who stands with his best friend by the priest. He is guileless and proud, the most virtuous among us, the most forgiving. He beams with love. It is he who reminds us who we are in the eyes of God.

Surrounding Beata, we walk her toward her destiny, this man who has parents and cousins and brothers and an aunt who's a nun. Lionel, who is not scandalized by the appearance in broad daylight of such women as we. He is fearless. It's love that gives him this courage, and he radiates it.

Earlier we prepared the bride, bathed, massaged, kissed, licked, fondled, gently bit, caressed, anointed her with oils, wove strands of cultured pearls and gladiola blooms into her hair, painted her toenails the colour of her inner labia—the exact shade of rose umber. We wrapped her in silk, drew feathers over her nipples, blessed her in every way we could think of.

She emerged as if from a Temple of Love, a new woman, ready for her bridegroom. In another time, there would have been prayers to Aphrodite ("gold-crowned and beautiful ... clothed in heavenly garments") and Hera (Queen of Immortals). But here in New France, in our hearts we murmur hymns to Holy Mary, Mother of God, Fountain of Beauty, Woman Transformed, Clothed with the Sun, Crowned with Stars, Joy of Israel, Queen of Love, Mother of Good Counsel, Most Wise, Most Powerful, Gentle in Mercy, Mirror of Justice, Throne of Wisdom, Mystical Rose, Tower of Ivory, House of Gold, Morning Star, Refuge of Sinners. Queen of Peace, pray for us, pray for us sinners, now and at the hour of our death.

The following June, Père Phillippe is harder to convince. He says he cannot, will not say Mass for a suicide, nor permit Beata's body to be buried in consecrated ground.

"Unthinkable," he says. "An abomination."

He says a great many stupid things and will not listen to reason, and so we come back late that night, Lionel and his friends bearing the body in a pine box they have made.

The day before, we cut her down from the rafter, removed the noose from her broken neck. Weeping and praying, we bathed the body, wrapped her in a sheet, placed, as best we could, flowers in her hands ... remembering when we had anointed her with oils, woven strands of pearls and blossoms in her hair. Our rage is equal only to our grief, and we proceed in silence to the rectory.

I pull the bell, pound on the door. The light goes on. Père Phillippe appears first at the upstairs window, leans out, tells us to go away. Then he notices how many of us there are. He notices the torches the men carry, perhaps realizes how quickly the rectory would burn to the ground, how difficult and awkward the explanations might be. When he opens the door a crack, we force ourselves in. He hands the keys to the chapel to one of the men, who goes in to open the door so Beata's coffin can be brought in. They light the candles. Père Phillippe says this is an outrage, says he will call the police. He has to be restrained, gagged. I draw my face close to his, tell him what is an outrage and what is not. From my bag, I pull a carving knife. Père Phillippe's eyes get quite large. He shakes his head, closes his eyes, and tears begin to squeeze out of them. When I pull up his dressing gown, I see he has pissed himself. When asked if he intends to cooperate, he nods yes, and yes, he will not cry out. I tell the men to go clean him up and get him dressed.

I step outside and vomit.

When the men have dressed Père Phillippe in his alb and cincture and cope, they lead him to the back door, where he greets the coffin with holy water and says the De Profundis and the Miserere.

"Jesus Christ, King of Glory, deliver the soul of the faithful departed."

"She has a name," I interrupt. "Say it."

"Beata," he says, his voice trembling. "Jesus Christ, King of Glory, deliver the soul of your faithful servant Beata from Hell. Lead her, St. Michael, into the holy Light. May light eternal shine on her. May the sacrifice of the Mass purify her. In the name of the Holy Lord, I grant absolution to

Beata." Here his voice catches, his eyes fill with tears, and he continues: "*Kyrie eleison; Christe eleison; Kyrie eleison.*"

When it comes time for the Pater Noster, Père Phillippe circumambulates the coffin, first with holy water and then incense.

"May the angels lead you into Paradise: may the martyrs receive you at your coming and lead you into the holy city, Jerusalem. May the choir of angels receive you, and with Lazarus, who once was poor, may you have everlasting rest."

We continue into the graveyard, where the men have nearly finished digging the grave that they'd begun even before we arrived. We must see this through to the end, must not allow Père Phillippe to lose heart, to change his mind. We must hold him to his vows. The men lower her coffin into the soft pungent earth. Père Phillippe leads us in the final prayers. Then we stand silent, all of us at peace for a moment, before we leave the graveyard in silence and go our separate ways.

One night after the war, a German industrialist came to the house and wanted to be flogged, and I wouldn't. He confessed his complicity with the Nazis. He described atrocities. He handed me the flogger.

He begged me.

I declined.

I wasn't angry; I simply wasn't interested. I had the sense that he'd told these stories to other women, and they'd obliged him. I had no investment in his remorse, but it was more than that. I felt obstinate in my refusal to punish him.

"You are already forgiven," I said.

He became furious, slapped me across the face. I gazed back at him with perfect equanimity, which only enraged him further. He grabbed my neck, pushed his thumbs into

my throat. I made no effort to scream. Nor did I struggle.
He might have murdered me on the spot. At that moment,
I realized what happens when you take away a punishing
God. When you love the way Christ loved, they want to
murder you. I have no idea what he saw in my eyes, but he
let me go, pushed me onto the bed, left the room and then
the house, and never came back.

It's February. Today I look out at the strange light reflected off
the snow. It has spring in it, this light, but spring is months
away. For weeks now, I have been unable to get to the studio.
Not because of the snow, but a strange lethargy. A friend tells
me I should consult my physician about depression. I tell her
it's remembering. Or not remembering. Maybe it's the end
of memory. I stare at objects. My mind is blank. This bright
blankness, the strange light off snow. Lead white. And not a
sound. No thread to connect one thought to another, and yet
one feels oneself to be in another time. The future? Again?
I spend long stretches of the day like this.

    I am not in any danger. That much is clear to me. But I
cannot paint or read or write and have no will—nothing to
drive me to do anything. It's quite pleasant, really. A kind
of dream. Maybe this is a form of forgiveness, when one
forgets what it was that was to be forgiven.

    I'm thinking about the war, how it began long before
anyone recognized its beginning and how it has lasted right
up to this moment, for it is the same war. Southeast Asia.
Central America. The Middle East. I'm thinking of how it is
like a forest fire that seems to be under control in one area,
only to break out in another, and how even when there seems
to be nothing left of the woods, it goes on burning in the
root system. I think of the war burning along our nerves,
something generated from the lizard part of our brain, a

nightmare that slithers and spits and scurries back into a hole in the earth.

Well into my forties, I continue to join the Bishop at the house for supper on Monday evenings from time to time. There's a Vietnamese girl who's become his favourite. Do`an Vien. She prepares soups with noodles and potatoes, chicken and scallions. We start out eating with chopsticks and do pretty well, then eat with our hands the chicken that does not fall off the bone, licking the spiced fat off our fingers, laughing. The flavours are more subtle than Chinese or Indian cuisine.

Her French is nearly flawless, and soon, under the Bishop's tutelage, she will speak very good English as well.

"Are you jealous?" he asks me.

"A little," I admit, but not in the way he assumes. I imagine her breast lifting toward the grazing light touch of my palm, her back arched, her mons rising to meet my lips ...

She is lovely, her face as placid and astonished as the moon. She walks with a limp, which makes her beauty all the more compelling.

"Shrapnel," the Bishop explains when she's out of the room. "A land mine. The war."

"*Une autre?*" I say. Another one?

"Don't you watch TV or read the papers?" he laughs.

"Never," I say. "*Jamais.*"

"Oh, you artists!" he says, leaning over to cradle my face in his ample palm.

I smile. I am lying, of course. I know all about it. I know people who are harbouring the young men from the States, trying to find them safe housing in the West.

"The Americans bombed her village," he continues. "Her parents, cultivated people, both doctors, were killed, and somehow she ended up here with Arienne."

"Grâce à Dieu!" I say. "She could have ended up with the dark sisters." Though the orphanage is long gone.

When I return to the studio, I cannot seem to paint anything but faces. No matter how hard I try to stick to abstraction, they emerge, disembodied at first, floating—Beata, Lionel, Arienne. Not portraits so much as a swirl of black cloud, a wave spilling mangled figures onto a foreign shore. And out of that, a kind of yellow ochre resurrection. They begin to take form, stand upright, demand to be in relation to one another. Seated at a table, they turn toward and away from one another. A bowl appears. An empty plate. A window in the background. The slice of an eave or dormer. Around them walls of crooked rooms assemble themselves. They are cartoons, disturbing in their serenity and in the questions that seem to hang in the air between us.

La crise d'Octobre, the October Crisis, 1970.
> Kidnappings.
> A murder that the FLQ calls an execution.
> The War Measures Act.
> Police, troops everywhere.
> And above our heads—helicopters.
> Not Vietnam. Here. *Chez nous.*

Somehow I have walked through this before. As a girl, when I escaped from the orphanage. I know how to do this, how to have no feeling and, now that I am a woman of a certain age, how to be gracious and patient with the young policemen and soldiers in the streets. And so I am allowed to go about my business, with no thought about where my sympathies lie. I simply continue along the way that has opened before me all my life and which today leads to the market, to my studio, to the *bateau ivre*.

I feel the tension in the air, and yes, the house is searched. We may be harbouring enemies of the State. We are not, of course, as they soon find out. And it's not as though the local chief of police hasn't known about us all these years. In fact, our good reputation is what allows us to stay open during the crisis, provides us with police protection at the opening of the *ruelle*, a young officer who checks identification before men pass through to the house. Even so, Arienne is beside herself with worry. She is irritable and short-tempered, and no one, save the Bishop, seems to be able to reassure her.

We live as we have always lived, day by day, only more so.

Something about the crisis sharpens our senses, by bringing the possibility of death closer, for we don't know where the FLQ might be in Quebec City, which apartments might be employed as bomb factories, what postbox might blow up next.

The Bishop dies suddenly in late November. Of a broken heart, I suspect, a casualty of the October Crisis, though the newspapers say it's a stroke.

That's how I find out, the newspaper.

The RCMP surround the Anglican Cathedral, checking everyone's papers because we are under martial law. I have no driver's license, so I bring along the deed to my apartment buildings and the new health insurance card with its blue *fleur-de-lys*. A formality. No one, I believe, is prevented from entering. The police are courteous, respectful.

But nervous.

Everyone is nervous.

The church is full. Because I am late, there is no room at the back, and so I sit somewhere in the middle. I feel strange, and yet I'd feel stranger not attending. I wear my best and

simplest black dress, a small black hat, black gloves. There
is no showing off today.

I don't see Arienne or any of the girls, which I understand, but it pains me. They stay away out of respect, perhaps.
I can only imagine Arienne's grief.

Then I see her, the Vietnamese girl, Do`an Vien. She
looks lost, so I stand and beckon her to sit beside me. She is
the image of my own grief, tiny and confused and walking
with her limp.

When she enters the pew, we clutch one another. She's
trembling. We hold hands through the long service, both
of us weeping quietly.

We walk back to the house together, and as I stand in
the front hallway, pulling off my gloves, I am surrounded
by the other girls.

"Where's Arienne?" I say.

Upstairs in her room, they say. "She won't see anyone.
But you, Thérèse. You must go to her and bring her down.
She hasn't taken any food for days."

"Let her be," I say and sit down to a simple meal with
them, describing the funeral as best I can.

Do`an Vien won't leave my side. She is mute, inconsolable.
I keep holding her hand and eat with the other.

She will not join in the meal.

All of us know this will mean something to the house,
but we cannot know what. We suspect the worst, that we
will close, that this is the end of us.

After supper, I go upstairs and knock softly at Arienne's
door.

"It's Thérèse."

There's no answer. I turn the knob and press, but the
door is barred.

I go back downstairs, instruct one of the other girls to

put Do'an Vien to bed and another to take her some warm milk and brandy when she's settled.

When I return to the house some weeks later, the parlour is full of boxes and suitcases. I find Arienne in her room, the door open.

"*Eh bien. Tu t'en vas?*"

"*Evidemment,*" she replies, not bothering to stop.

"Arienne. Turn around. Look at me!"

"The dream is over, Thérèse. It's time to wake up."

"Who will run the household?"

"What household? The house has been put up for sale. We must all be out by Monday."

I go to the open armoire and touch one of the gowns.

"And these?"

"Of what use will they be to me in Saint-Honoré?"

"Why Saint-Honoré?"

"My sister is ill. She needs me. I'll find some peace there."

"But how will you manage?"

"Do you think you're the only one the Bishop felt obligated to?"

"I'm sorry. Of course."

"But the other girls aren't so lucky. They must fend for themselves. They'll manage."

"And Do'an Vien?"

"Gone. I don't know where. It's no concern of mine."

"Arienne!"

"There's no time for sentimentality, Thérèse. We're lucky not to be in jail. Now please. I have work to do."

I step toward her, turn her around. She looks worn out. She has grown old.

"You took me in, gave me a home."

"You owe me nothing, Thérèse. What more do you want of me?"

"I can't bear to think of you in Saint-Honoré."

"You think too much, *chérie*. You always did." And here she softens, smiles.

She touches my face. "Take care of yourself, Thérèse. *Adieu*."

The house, it turns out, was owned by the Bishop, as I suspected. My properties, he had signed over to me long before he died. I imagine he's done something similar for Arienne, so that his will would not be contested.

I never find out what became of Do`an Vien. She simply vanished. I ask around for months, stop short of going to the police. I fear she has been sent back to Vietnam, where the war still rages.

Blissfully ill, I sink. I touch bottom and rise again. After the struggle, the holding on or holding away, I dissolve and am released from paralysis. My bed rises, floats through the doorway as if in my mother's drowned village. This other kind of gravity. I rise and am pulled sideways, from room to room, without any clear notion of why. When I sit at the table to write in my notebook, the script unravels under my pen and rises like sand caught in an updraft. A narrative—two, five, hundreds of stories—unwinding like balls of string, haphazard, one long dirty strand after another, following with momentum and then lying there, somehow connecting everything that is.

I have started to fall—like a dry leaf from a very high branch.

Not the kind of falling one does when one is young.

Not sudden.

Not falling in love.

Not falling apart.

I have started to fall—to earth. Started to land like a meteor, in slow motion—falling until I land, and in landing, I create the crater of my own grave.

I dream of a slim house alongside the one I live in, with people going about their business. I am invisible in the dream—they have no sense whatsoever that I am there. At first, I move aside to let them pass to put plates on the kitchen table, but I needn't.

They walk right through me. I have the density of clean air, lighter than mist, and yet I can see it all, hear their voices as echoing whispers in a language I can neither speak nor identify, yet seem to understand.

The language of the dead, perhaps.

Or the way human language sounds to angels.

Theo

When did I first notice Theo's gaze? It might have been snowing, and I think Beethoven was on the radio. I may have been modelling for a drawing class. I seem to remember plaster dust, greyish light. I moved myself into the positions I was directed to take by the professor. I sat, turned a bit, with my hands in my lap, looking out the window at bare branches, so it must have been late autumn. Or I might have been in a café, talking to others. What I remember is looking elsewhere, when I felt something like heat in its intensity. And then this awareness of a presence, as if he'd walked up and stood right beside me. I looked around, trying to find out what it was, and it took a minute or two before I found Theo, who by then had averted his gaze. But it was he who had been staring, and I knew it.

What I don't remember is the first time we actually spoke. I must have been the one to initiate it. And the subject of the conversation has also escaped my memory. Which is odd, really. I remember in exact detail the moment I first met the Bishop and any number of other lovers. But Theo—it's as if he somehow insinuated himself, with great stealth, past every guard and barrier, until he stood in my chamber, breathless with the effort it took, surprised that he'd actually come this far.

"Who are you?" I might have said. "And how did you get in?" I wasn't annoyed or frightened, just astonished.

Beethoven on the radio. I might have asked him what was playing, and he might have said one of the later sonatas. Or he might not have known. Or it might not have been Beethoven at all. And not snowing. But once he'd arrived, it was as if he'd always been there, wearing wool trousers and a jacket. A Basque beret. A dusty white shirt, smudged with paint. Theo was meticulous, even obsessive, about hygiene, but work in the studio was work—hard, physical work. Never mind the kind of psychic strain under which Theo always laboured.

Thin and lithe, full of nervous energy, quixotic, yet always slightly pulling back whatever he'd just put forward. Hesitant. Unsure. With sudden great bouts of passionate certainty, as though once he had pushed past the hindrance in his thinking, there was no stopping him. Later, he suffered agonies of shame and self-doubt, but then he'd start up again. I picture him poised to run at a bully, head down, ready to butt him like a goat. In this way his thought progressed beyond what any of the rest of us were capable of thinking on our own. Yet we followed him, hesitant in our own ways, never quite certain of the line we were following, arguing, as my people do, always arguing about *le mot juste*, the words to say it.

August 1948. Theo ran into the café with an illustrated booklet in his hand, from which he read aloud, without sitting down:

> *Le règne de la peur multiforme est terminé ...*
>> *The reign of fear in all its forms is over ...*
>> *fear of prejudice—fear of public opinion—of persecutions ...*
>> *peur d'être seul sans Dieu ...*
>> *peur de soi—de son frère—de la pauvreté*
>> *fear of the established order—of ridiculous justice*
>> *fear of new relations;*
>> *fear of the irrational;*
>> *fear of necessities;*
>> *fear of floodgates opening on one's faith in man—on the society of the future;*
>> *fear of forces able to release transforming love ....*

"At last," he said. "Borduas dares to print what we think."

And it was true. This document voiced something already in the air between us, in the studio, in the cafés—our most intimate unarticulated longings. We were pushing against something—the Church, to be sure—and something else we were becoming more and more aware of but couldn't name. The State, English Canada, our legacy of shame and ignorance, a holding back, not quite taking a full breath. And here the air rushed into our lungs.

Theo continued to read:

> *Remove the motivation of competition for raw materials, prestige and authority, and nations might live*

harmoniously. But grant supremacy to whom you wish,
give world control to whom you please, and the same
deep-rooted patterns will emerge—although perhaps with
different details.

They signify the end of Christian civilization.

"*Hérésie!*" someone shouted. "*La sédition!*"

"At last! It's about time!" someone else said.

"*Communiste!*" another cried out.

People brought their chairs in from the sidewalk. We made room for them. The waiters stopped serving and stood, listening, perplexed.

"*Pas du tout communiste!*" shouted a broad-shouldered man, who stood up and took the floor. "There's no program here, no analysis. This is a dream with no plan, no real way forward."

"*Ta gueule! Laisse-le continuer!*"

The large man sat down.

Theo continued:

Magic booty, magically wrested from the unknown, lies at
our feet. It has been gathered by the true poets. Its power
to transform is measured by the violence shown against
it and by its resistance in the end to exploitation.

Still looking skeptical, the communist nevertheless leaned forward and listened.

My attention was divided. I was transfixed by what Theo was reading, yet I couldn't take my eyes off the handsome, broad-shouldered man who had interrupted. I'd never seen him before. He seemed to be alone.

Make way for magic! ...

PLACE AUX MYSTÈRES OBJECTIFS!
PLACE À L'AMOUR!
PLACE AUX NÉCESSITÉS!

"Comrades!" The brawny man stood up again. "The necessities are material! Without clear objectives, your revolution is doomed to fail. Read Marx!"

"To hell with Marx!"

"To hell with you!"

"Sit down. Let him finish."

Some cheered. A few stormed out of the café. Others moved their chairs closer.

And above the din, Theo's voice continued reading the document till the end.

What followed was silence. Not even the handsome communist knew what to say. Gradually, people got up to leave, some stopping for a word with Theo on their way out. The waiters gathered the cups and glasses and started pulling in the tables from the terrace.

In the end there were three of us left. Theo, myself, and—oddly enough—Renard, the communist.

"My little man," he said to Theo. "Be reasonable. I sympathize with much of what you had to say, but really, there are practical concerns. Surely you don't imagine the ruling class will roll over and let you stroke its tummy, now, do you?"

I could see that Theo was exhausted. I was insulted on Theo's behalf, but also intrigued by this stranger, who seemed to be flirting with me—through Theo. Looking back, I see that he was seducing us both.

I was twenty-two, and often more interested in my power over men than in the men themselves. Despite my own vanity, I felt compelled to protect Theo, who dreamed not so much of a revolution as a new *atelier*, colleagues willing to search with him for the language that would describe this new reality.

Yes, I stayed because I thought Renard might walk me home. But I was also drawn by something deeper. Something about the words themselves and Theo's voice made me feel I had come home. A place for me at last, not just to reside, but to help build. Ultimately, I stayed because I heard the *Refus Global* in the same way Theo had: something that was already in me, struggling for voice, struggling to appear on the canvas, struggling to transform my life and the world itself, a world and self that had already appeared.

Renard walking me home. Did I really think that? Would I have allowed him to, had he asked? I lived in two distinct worlds that never overlapped. L'École des beaux-arts, where I modelled for the students Thursdays and Saturdays and sometimes painted with Theo after hours; and the house where I'd lived since I was fourteen, under the supervision of Arienne and the Anglican Bishop. Instinct rather than any fear of judgment told me to keep them separate. I wonder now. By the time I was twenty-two, I'd developed a stealthy discretion as graceful as any spy's. For I could pass between worlds—this one and that.

Secular and sacred.

Public and private.

English and French.

I wasn't stupid. I knew I could be arrested at almost any moment for nearly anything you can think of. Simply listening to something like the *Refus Global* in those days. Never mind that I had no birth certificate, that I'd run away from the orphanage and was living in a *bordel*. My situation was tenuous at best. That I existed at all was most likely against somebody's law. And yet here I was.

This new world after the war. How rich in complexity it grows. When not at *le bateau ivre*, I am painting or modelling at the art school or out with Theo and Renard. We become a mysterious "item" among the other students. They are a little scandalized. Also interested. Envious, perhaps. We are three points of a triangle that keeps changing shape, though more often than not, Theo and I form the base. Or so I imagine.

Renard and Theo spend time together and exclude me. I know they are lovers even when I am not present. I try to feel what it is between men—and cannot. What I can't quite grasp is their conversation. What can they possibly have to talk about when I am not there? For between Theo and me there is a constant stream of thought and inquiry that often exasperates Renard, and he goes off somewhere on his own. But what do they talk about when they are alone together? Politics, I imagine. And I imagine Theo straining to enter the mind of Marxist dialectic, something that Renard himself isn't really clear about. For Renard it's more to do with resentments against the rich, an old tribal hatred that lives in all of us.

Theo and I belong to a different tribe, or a different family of the same tribe, and I begin to feel the pulling apart of two poles: the artists and intellectuals who will become the new politicians, and the street fighters. Looking back, I might have known that even then, embodied as the conflict seemed to be in Theo and Renard. Their difficult exchanges, their heated animal coupling, their desire for one another and the growing frustration that would one day result in a kind of contempt. Which seemed to fuel the erotic charge between them. Until it didn't.

Today the only thing that really frightens me is a blank canvas. Absurd, after the real dangers I've faced. A blank canvas can stop me in my tracks for weeks at a time. It's a complex of some sort. I suspect it has something to do with what was beginning to show itself in a previous painting. For it shows itself to me, the painting. It's out of my control. Of course I decide to begin it, but then I step away and am often stupefied by how the painting unfolds.

When I close my eyes, I see a crack of light, as if through a wall, a fissure of light between two darker shapes. I want to know about the lines that describe the edges and depth, the inwardness of the fissure, and the relationship of the bright light between the lines and the pale wash outside the lines.

Yet what difference can it possibly make? When I look at the world around me—as war rages and famine spreads—I doubt the validity of painting at all.

I am walking with Theo through the fields that stretch from the mental hospital to the convent in Charlesbourg. He tells me that, as a teenager, he was hospitalized because he became crazy. That's how he says it. We imagine them as interchangeable, the convent and the madhouse. One small blasphemy after another escapes our lips as we part shoulder-high wheat and lie down to make love—under their very noses. I imagine the nuns can smell our sweat, a perfume that drives them wild with an obscure, unnameable pleasure. Dark and musky. "The earth," they might say, catching it in the breeze. Or they might say something about the season and God's bounty. They will think of the coming harvest and Thanksgiving, when underneath there is this incalculable longing—for God, they suppose. Or for a man, or each other, or revenge—a knife through the heart of their abbess. I'm surprised at my anger, aware of how it fuels our lovemaking there in the field.

Theo comes into me savagely, more so here than when

we are in bed. He must sense it too, this extra heat, his own fear, the excitement, as if …

"*Tabernac!*" he cries out in a hoarse whisper as he comes.

And I smile.

To defile the Church with love is more delicious than a bomb or a general strike. To risk everything—shame, excommunication, imprisonment, torture, martyrdom—for love, for God, for men—is something these sisters in their stiff, black cotton will never understand.

Then another kind of excitement overtakes me—the thought of scythes, the men on tractors, cutting the wheat and finding us there. Then an image of my father's body in pieces, sliced by the threshing machine, and I push Theo off me. "*Ah ben maudite marde!*"

I pull myself to my knees, gather my skirt and sweater over my breasts.

"*Qu'est-ce que tu as?*"

"*Rien.*" I pull up my panties, crouched below the top of the wheat, pull on my skirt, my blouse, my sweater.

"*Vite. Vite,*" I say, and pull him to his feet. He hops from one foot to the other, pulling on his trousers. I drag him onto the road that divides the fields and march him back toward town. It's a long way. We'll follow the river.

"What?" he says. "What is it? What did you see? Was it your father?"

But how can he know? At what point did I tell him? Certainly not in one of these moments of panic—so wild with fear that I cannot speak.

Then I remember. It was in the studio I told Theo how my father died. We were looking at one of my paintings, a nightmare, and there it was, somehow in the movement of the paint. Theo asked and I told him how my father had died, in a thresher, at harvest time in a field near my mother's village that was later drowned by the hydroelectric dam.

The next day, I force myself back into the studio. I begin by cleaning up. Straightening, putting things away. Rearranging what I've already organized. It has been too long, and we are hostile, cautious with one another, these paintings and I. And these blank canvases, the idle brushes, the jar of spirits, silent, yellow, accusing. Dried paint on the palette must be scraped off. I had left as if fleeing a scene of ruin to which I would never return.

I start with cadmium yellow, an extravagant choice. It's expensive and I know it will be covered. I can't help myself. It's the first colour I reach for. Impulse. No thought. Then it strikes me: I'm burying gold under red ochre, cobalt, burnt umber. With my palette knife, I dig into what has become thick mud and reclaim the cadmium yellow. Layers. Seeing through the layers—as though I were diving into the earth this time, not a river—I discover a slow flux, a rhythm that we mistake for solidity.

Flowers. They're painting flowers at the art school. Theo shows me, and I practise from his paintings. I have nothing against flowers, but if I paint them, I want them to be in the garden, alive, still connected to their roots.

They draw the figure from plaster statues—from Europe. The students are told how lucky they are, how expensive the plasters are, how careful they must be. Only the professors and certain privileged students are allowed to move them. I want to smash them, smash them all, then rip my clothes from my body, rip the clothes from Renard's massive body, and say to them, "Paint this. Look at us. Look at each other, the bodies you desire and dream about."

I want us all to take our clothes off and sketch each other in turn. I want the professor to be naked too. All of us. Nothing to hide.

Usually I am the only one who is nude, sitting demurely, looking out the window into the grey between bare branches or snow or budding leaves as the academic year comes to a close.

On Saturdays, I pose in robes made from old bed sheets, pose as an angel or as the Virgin Mary for the priests who take drawing classes.

I began painting as a joke to see if the professors at the École could tell my work from Theo's. At first I took all the assignments Theo was given and tried them myself, patterning myself on Theo's style, imitating it. Then we both began experimenting with abstraction, following Picasso at first, and then following our own instincts and the paint itself. Without knowing it, we were doing what the Automatistes were doing, and it wasn't until we heard of them that it occurred to us that anyone else in Quebec was doing it too. We were beside ourselves with excitement.

What prevented me from attending the École des beaux-arts? I couldn't come through the front door of anything—not after the orphanage—for fear of becoming trapped. And so I snuck in the back way, painted in the studios when they were vacant.

They say Georgia O'Keeffe's paintings of flowers are really of vulvas. They say the petals are labia, the stamen is the clitoris. I wonder. Is my vulva a flower? Are my labia petals? I shudder to think of how easily they would tear. People who speak this way do violence to both flower and vulva, as if they'd sliced them up and put them between glass slides under a microscope. But when I think of what Theo calls the trumpet lilies, with raindrops sliding down the walls of the bloom, it's as if my own throat were open to the heavens, filling with rainwater. That feels different. I don't know what the painter herself says about the paintings. If she says anything at all, it has not reached us here in Quebec. And this may be another reason I avoid conscious "image." Interpretation leads nowhere but away from the painting itself.

Today, I am surrounded by prepared canvases, all of them square for some reason. What was I thinking when I bought them? I confess, I sometimes begin with imagery, then cover it over, let the image dissolve beyond its own edges. I confess I sometimes long to paint a mountain, the river, your face in firelight, a hyacinth. This other thing I am doing wears me out. And when I sit before the blank canvas, I know why. These paintings are how my destiny makes itself known to me. It was Theo who first suggested it.

"What if they are from the future?" he said.

"The future?"

"Why not?"

And so we began a series of experiments in clairvoyance, shall we say.

Theo sat down, and I began to paint him. Whenever I'd get distracted by his face, I'd close my eyes and continue painting. Soon I followed only what was happening on the canvas, looking up from time to time at Theo, who sat remarkably still, staring at a fixed point somewhere in the distance.

I turned the picture around and pulled up a chair beside Theo.

"Ah!" he said. "I am going on a long journey. And there's some difficulty, maybe even bloodshed."

He pointed to a smear of red toward the upper right corner.

I laughed, and then we both grew silent.

"And there we are, the three of us," he said. "That triangle."

"Which one is Renard?" I asked.

"Here," he said, indicating the point furthest from the other two.

"And are you alone on this journey?"

"Yes," he said, staring at the painting. "Apparently so."

"Now you paint me," I said.

He put a stretched canvas on the easel and began with three broad strokes. I tried not to watch him, though it didn't really matter where I turned my gaze. Staccato jabs. A gesture like scribbling. Then larger arched movements.

Theo painted like a man possessed. He looked to be in physical pain, his face in a grimace. He moved in like a fencer, like a picador, with his brushes, and then danced back out of the way as if the canvas were about to charge at him. Painting was an act of war to him sometimes and sometimes a languid loving, but always with this tension, this urgency.

At last he turned the easel around and joined me to look at it.

"What do you see?" he asked.

There was no fixed point. Nothing was still. Everything moving. A kind of spiral that seemed to expand and contract at the same time.

"Many loves," he said. "And a secret." He pointed to a section in which one shape partially obscured another.

I looked at him.

"Let's paint Renard!" I said.

"It probably won't work," said Theo. "He's not here."

We tried anyway, turning a long canvas on its side and

placing it on the easel. And to work we went, moving over each other, back and forth, until I stopped.

"You're cheating! There's an image."

We stepped back, and sure enough, there was the shaft and head of an enormous phallus.

"The future, indeed!" cried Theo, as he grabbed me, moving toward the daybed, and we made love.

Theo was so much like the god Pan, I sometimes checked for cloven hooves. He was not hairy anywhere but on his legs and his buttocks. He was of another world, the animals or something else, not entirely us. Sometimes, holding him, I felt as if I were holding him to the earth against his will. I could almost feel him leap, lift straight up and away from me. Sometimes, even now, I hear his voice, but not his human voice, a single note, high, beautiful as in a boys' choir—just a single note and then another, not far from it—one long note and then another and another, stepping clearly from one tone to a minor tone to something else. Never sliding. Never wavering.

Sa tendresse. That's what I'm thinking about this evening. And his body, all fur below the waist and smooth and boyish above. His black eyebrows and curly black hair—long as an archangel's. Feminine even with the dark shadow of his beard. His hands, small and intent, full of the energy of his paintings, where animal and mind met, as in love. Without words, so there was not the hesitation or the stumbling to find the right way to express ideas that had no place in our world. In love he would gaze at me, as if about to pose some question that would sometimes be spoken days later in the street or the studio and seem to come from nowhere, but I think it had occurred to him while making love, sometimes with the two of us.

How was it for Renard, making love with Theo—or Theo, making love with Renard? Theo seemed to make no distinction between us in those moments, darting his mouth from one to another, his eyes alive, playful, curious to see what new heights of pleasure or passion he could rouse in us, and then he'd watch, circling us when Renard and I coupled and he'd cup my buttocks in his huge hands and grind and push and lift me higher and higher, my back arched, my legs spread over his thighs as he knelt, and Theo circling like a wind, like a fire that played all around our bodies, until we all lay in a heap, panting, sometimes laughing, Theo and I sometimes crying.

"Women," Renard would say to both of us, and turn away.

Handsome, arrogant, feisty: that's what we loved about Renard, Theo and I. And that he could turn away, which Theo and I seemed incapable of doing. And his massive thighs and chest—his arms that could enfold us both. Tall, broad, hairy, with his briny, intoxicating odour. We were so small next to him.

People often thought he was our *jules*, or mine at least. And we played that out at night sometimes—for protection. No one would want to tangle with my pimp or my pimp's little pal.

It's a snowy Monday. We've been playing in bed all night, dozing. We are sleepy and stupefied by sex, wondering what there is to eat, and if there's coffee, and who will go out for milk. There's money, no rent to pay. The Bishop has bought the building and put the deed in my name. Renard has the day off from building cabinets because he and his father have worked all weekend. The art school is still not in session because of the holiday, but later, Theo and I will be painting. We have this morning open before us. We lie in one another's arms, with the luxury of wondering and deciding what's next.

"What shall we do?" says Renard. "What's the plan?"

"No plan, *s'il te plaît*, Renard. Let's stay like this," says Theo. "All day."

"I'm hungry," I say, stretching.

"Let's go out then," says Renard, "buy a paper, get something to eat."

"I'm not moving," says Theo. "You two go out and bring me something to eat. Surprise me. But no! I can't be without you for that long." He grabs Renard and pulls me closer. "Come here. Come here."

"*Arrête*," says Renard, without much energy. "*Ça suffit! J'en ai marre!*" He yawns. "*Les putes ne peuvent rien décider!*"

"Don't insult us," says Theo. "We're artists, not whores."

"Whores, artists, what's the difference?" shrugs Renard.

"All right then, *Camarade* Renard!" says Theo, standing up on the bed. "I delegate you as Supplies Commissioner. Go find us some coffee, *une baguette, de la confiture, et un journal. Vite! Vite!* What are you waiting for? I gave you an order. Why, this is insubordination!"

Renard simply puts out his hand.

"Money," I say, getting up to fetch my pocketbook.

"And Thérèse and I shall perform shameless, revolutionary acts of Free Love, striking another blow against bourgeois marriage, until you come back with provisions."

"Useless anarchists. You wouldn't recognize the revolution if it came and sat on your face!" Renard mutters, pulling on trousers, boots, and his *tuque* as he heads out the door.

"*Sois sage, mon vieux!* I'll report you to the Politburo, and then where will you be?" cries Theo, laughing.

But Renard is already halfway down the stairs.

Renard is right, of course. We have no plan for how we

are to proceed. Theo and I follow instinct and feeling. As if he and I have exchanged a vow we recognize only later as having occurred the night of the *Refus Global*. We are a threesome, but it is Theo and I who share our dreams and our days, painting, talking. We take endless walks and sit in cafés waiting for Renard to join us. And when he does, Theo and I light up; we adore him, and cannot get enough of him. Yet Renard cannot follow us on the path we are cutting through the wilderness.

It's the end-of-year banquet at the art school. June 1949. Theo and I wear black suits; my hair is tucked up under a bowler hat and he carries a cloth flower. On my upper lip, I have drawn a thin moustache with an oil crayon. We have come as Apollinaire, poet and muse, though we explain this to no one.

"And who are you?" asks a student dressed as a lumberjack.

"The angels the angels in the sky," I say. "One's dressed as an officer / One's dressed as a chef today."

"Mellifluent moon on the lips of the maddened," says Theo. "The orchards and towns are greedy tonight / The stars appear like the image of bees."

He pinches the man's arm and we move on ...

"Say who you are!" cries a Spanish dancer.

"The rose floats at the water's edge," answers Theo. "The maskers have passed by in crowds."

"It trembles in me like a bell," I say. "This heavy secret you ask now."

And we move on.

When anyone asks us a question, we answer with a poem, whatever comes to mind. Sometimes he begins and I complete it. Sometimes I begin and he either completes it or makes a gesture and remains silent.

This year, the menu is written in such a way as to include the nicknames of the students and professors. The war is over, and we are in high spirits. Someone recites Rabelais:

> *Le mal temps passe et retourne le bon,*
> *Pendant qu'on trinque autour de gras jambon.*

Another recounts an anecdote. Theo laughs so hard, he has to bury his face in the shawl of Francine, who sits next to him. Claudette wears a fez whose black tassel swings back and forth as she laughs. Even Renard, dressed as *le salaud*, softens into parody and play, and I can see something of the boy he once was, despite the blue-black shadow along his jaw.

Ambition, politics, aesthetic differences, ideology, resentments are all set aside as we toast Pellan and our other teachers, Borduas, who was fired from the École du meuble for writing the *Refus Global*, even Duplessis, the Devil himself, we toast, and then toast the melted snow and hyacinths and the moon.

I am suddenly full of nostalgia for the drafty drawing studios and overheated washrooms. I love the plaster dust, the banging and hissing radiators, the way in which tonight we have transformed the cavernous sculpture studio into a great hall for a sumptuous feast.

I am a little drunk, and Theo is more than a little drunk. In fact, he is being walked out, half-carried by a student dressed as the Queen of Sheba and a strong man in the circus. I know he's in good hands. Besides, I am dancing with Renard, who has kissed me and smudged my moustache. At what point do I decide to go home with Renard? And whom am I betraying? Which part of Apollinaire is betrayed? The muse or the poet? And who enacts the betrayal? And why is it even a question of betrayal?

Only later, when I see it in Theo's face, do I understand that I've hurt him. But how? *The reign of fear in all its forms is over.*

But not jealousy.

Yes, there was Riopelle. We knew of him. How could we not? The darling of Canadian abstract painters in Paris, driving race cars, drinking with the Surrealists. He was in the spotlight. We worked in the shadows. Theo mistrusted Riopelle's fame, his public antics, what Theo saw as his arrogance. He also, I think, secretly envied him for just those qualities. Yes, the photographs of Riopelle's work engaged us, and yet we were not drawn to follow him. We were not followers by nature, and soon *le petit mouvement*, which had seemed to be growing, simply petered out. Bourduas in New York and then Paris. Riopelle in the gossip columns.

Something in the pronouncements began to sound empty.

Theo felt he should go elsewhere, be in the thick of it—Paris or New York. And yet the land claimed him, the river claimed him, and for a long time he could not move.

We'd talk for hours after we painted, first sitting in silence, just looking, smoking, wondering what it was that could be emerging from the pigment. As with Theo, the land laid claim to me too, and I kept seeing it everywhere in our work. *No image. No past. No memory.* How was it possible? It began to seem to me another kind of tyranny. And yet we held to it as a discipline, a means of discovering something else about paint and what it could and could not express. So that we wouldn't be seduced by the sentimentality of landscape or figure. And yet that's all I kept seeing—landscape and figure. So I'd close my eyes, open them again, and see rhythm, colour, movement, gesture, dreaming—the future.

Back in the studio, I stare into a new painting.

The mud of March or April—blackish, brown—snow—mauves, violets, and a warm burnt umber shot through with orange—this rectangle, that area—nothing to hold them together—spillage—layering a pale tan under the violet—there is some gesture missing that I lack the courage for. My life as I've known it is pulling apart like paint that somehow contracts as it dries, recedes to open areas of blank canvas—the earthen riverbed of drought.

There. It's the earth after all—black, dormant, waiting for seed, for warmth, and wet—and not snow, but a luminosity. Where does it come from? There's no sun in the painting. The source of light is within, underneath, and yet I brushed it over with the mauve-violet—a gesture that somehow begins to draw the two ends back toward the centre.

When I move out of *le bateau ivre*, Theo and Renard are at my apartment, ready to help me unload my books and clothes from the *calèche*. We are full of false bravado. As if I have been released from some kind of prison, when in fact I've left the place where I cultivated my true liberty.

I am free to engage more openly in politics, to join picket lines and marches in the street.

But at dinner that evening, there is a new tension. The air feels thinner, as if we were at a new and dizzying altitude.

Finally, I break a long silence. *"C'est l'ange qui passe ..."* The angel passing. "This changes nothing! We'll go on as we have been."

I pour out more wine. "A toast! To our new freedom—unimaginable until this moment!"

Three glasses rise and touch lightly, but no one's eyes meet, and we finish the meal mostly in silence.

"What are you worried about? I will make the same

money. I'll continue to work at the house and model at the
art school. I still have my patron. Who knows? I may begin
to sell my paintings! Anything is possible. Anything!"

But something has happened. Something I don't know
about.

Renard leaves, claiming he has an early start in the
morning. And Theo follows.

I sit smoking at the kitchen table, finish the bottle of
wine, and then clear away the plates.

The first night of my new life, I sleep alone.

I meet Theo at the café some days later and find him listless,
evasive. When we go back to the apartment to make love, we
fumble with each other like teenagers. As if we are ashamed.
We are both frightened of something we cannot name.

Without Renard, we are incomplete, a three-legged stool
that can't stand on two.

He breaks down in my arms and sobs—long, strangled
fits of weeping.

I hold him and hold him, and then I know.

Renard has left the *ménage*. I can only guess the circumstances. A new girl. A fight with Theo. Or something about
me that Renard is unwilling to discuss.

Whatever has happened, we have both lost Renard.

And what Theo has felt all along for him was for him
alone—it never included me.

And what was between Theo and me that did not include
Renard?

I wonder.

Perhaps it was the two of them all along, and I was their
witness and protection.

Even painting together in the studio the next day, we
inhabit different countries. I am seized with the desire to

make a portrait of Theo—his face, his torso. His cock, his buttocks, the black triangle of hair at the sacrum. It's as if I want to gather up all of the parts of him that have been severed and strewn across a field.

I become obsessed with what I can no longer have—what is no longer mine.

When we stop painting and look, we are silent.

"I'm going away, Thérèse. It's no good for me here. I can't paint. I'm going to New York."

The world that I thought I knew is dissolving, bit by bit, and floating away.

I agree to store his paintings.

"You will always have a place here, Theo. You know that."

He nods.

"You'll write to me, won't you?"

We fall onto each other, like two animals fighting. We try to separate but cannot. Hungry enough to eat each other's flesh.

This is the way we make love for the last time.

After he leaves Quebec, Theo sends me postcards from New York City. The Statue of Liberty. The Empire State Building. On one he writes that he's found a studio to share with a boy from Belgium. On another that he's met someone called Betty Parsons at a wild party. He says she runs an important gallery. Another postcard says he has seen Jackson Pollock and de Kooning in a bar.

Names I recognize from *Life* magazine.

Not a word of how they paint, what they talk about, what they believe.

I long for a letter.

I can't write to him. He has given me no address.

I have no phone number to call.

The postcards come less and less frequently over the next few years, with simply *"Je t'embrasse"* or *"Grosses bises"* scrawled on the back.

Then late one night a knock at the door. Renard stumbles in, drunk. I lead him to a chair, and he weeps. I can't make sense of it. Theo. New York. A knife. A bar. An alley.

And then I understand.

Theo is dead.

There is not room in my apartment for anything but Renard's fury, his immense grief. The weight of it so ponderous, I cannot lift it. All I can do is to guide him to the couch and sit on the floor and smooth his ravaged face until he sleeps.

And then I go out walking.

I enter a church and sit in front of a statue of Sainte Thérèse. It is then that my waters break, as pregnant women say. Not birth, but the waters of anguish, remorse, desolation, and despair. A soundless keening for the one man in this world who I felt knew me.

It is dawn when I return from my walk, and Renard has disappeared. It is only then that I am capable of collapse, surrender, audible weeping.

I have lost everything—inspiration, friendship, my youth.

When I do finally sleep, I dream that I am standing beside a *rivière*, and then on a small, stone bridge. When I look down, I see a dog walking along the bottom, underwater, crossing to the other side, where Theo's frozen body begins to slip down the muddy bank.

I seem to wake and hear the sea pushing itself through a narrow place in the rocks far below me, at first harsh and then more and more soothing, until I sleep again and dream of seabirds circling and swooping high above the house where I still sleep and sink into the soft hiss and sucking of seawater far, far below.

I spend hours—days—in bed, staring up. I cannot bear the thought of carrying out the trash. I cannot endure another loss. I grow acquisitive in my mind. I hoard memories of Theo and move about my flat touching his objects again and again. Why are there so few of them? Why did they not seem to matter when he was still alive?

I dream I visit his family's house on the south shore. I am crazed with desire, pull flowers up by their roots, clutch them to my breasts. Once in the house I pick up spoons and put them in my pocket. I touch every piece of furniture and wonder how I can get it home with me. I want everything that ever came into contact with Theo, and I want it to belong only to me. Once out of the house and back in another part of the garden, I encounter my mother, laughing. She opens her fists, and pebbles and dirt fall out. In the dream I know she is right, and yet I grip the spoons in my pocket and feel utterly destitute.

Weeks later, I am up and about my studio, clearing away old things, tearing up drawings and putting them in the stove—old paintings, brushes, palette knives, charcoal—out, out, out. Everything out. I can't bear the sight of it. I stop short of burning the few paintings I have from Theo and these notebooks. And when I realize I had been about to burn them, I break down and weep.

In the mirror my face is haggard. I keep losing weight. I seem to be vanishing, becoming a ghost.

I see her again, the woman who will not eat. I recognize her from the bookstore on Saint-Jean. She worked there for years, and then disappeared. When I saw her, I nodded. She seemed not to recognize me, looked beyond, through me even, so I spoke her name and she turned. We stopped to talk. I wanted to ask her if she was dying, but of course I felt I couldn't.

"I've been ill," she said, with a knowing smile, faintly superior.

"I'm sorry," I said. "I hope you will be better."

But she won't be. She grows thinner and thinner. Cancer, I think. But later I am told it is a nervous disease of not eating that wastes her away. She has lost her appetite. I think of the thresher that ate my father. A death fitting to the Industrial Age. Its hunger. That a machine could have appetite, but not this woman. That a lack of appetite could eat us alive. Far more slowly than any war machine.

I myself have no appetite. I lie in bed for days, not sleeping, dreaming awake. All nightmares. Images of Theo dead, his dear face, staring, not staring, blank. Vacant. So much life. Then not. Beata. Faces I never painted. No portraits, no record, no memory. And yet here they are, well past midnight.

Not nostalgia. It's desire that returns when I finger the sleeve of a silk jacket in a shop. Not the object, but the sensation, the feel of it, the way it drapes and hangs and moves when I try it on and take a few steps along the dress shop floor.

"*C'est charmante,*" the saleswoman says.

I can imagine being desirable again in this jacket. I can imagine the admiring and hungry gaze of men on the Boardwalk, or along the Grande-Allée. I can imagine the touch of a man. I re-enter the world of desire through the sleeves of a beige silk jacket like magic. I begin to long for it, and would buy it right then and there, but it has nothing to do with the jacket, this desire. It is desire itself, reawakened by the smooth and buttery feel of the silk. Cool, seeming warm to the touch.

I thank the saleswoman and step back out into February—life stirring in my bones again.

The night the art school burned, I felt it in my body. The building had been abandoned for some time; the easels, paints, and platforms had of course already been moved to the new school. Kids, the newspaper said later. Or squatters. Not the FLQ. I'd gone to bed early and woken up with a fever, sweating, gasping for air. I looked around me, opened the window, listened. Nothing. No voices crying out. No sirens. In the dream, I might have been in the building. And yet I woke up without any sense of a particular place. It was my body that was aflame, from the inside. I drank some water. I took a bath. I dressed and went out to walk. Then I saw the clouds lit up, smoke, and I took off running. I stood with the others and watched it burn.

"Kids," someone said.

I'm forty-four, old enough to be their mother. All I can feel is numb, blank. And then every corner of the place comes back to me: the drawing and painting studios, the library, the stairways, lavatories, lockers, the plaster dust everywhere, the winters of grey light. And Theo in all of it.

It was Theo I most wanted to tell.

Weeks later, when they tear the rest of it down, I feel that, too, in my body. I knew of the plans, the new road, all that was to be torn down to make way for a convention centre, but it isn't until I feel it being pulled down in my own body that I really know. I am in bed for some days, feel every strike of the headache ball, the sledgehammer, hear from inside the groan of every beam, am choked by the dust, am conscious of every brick, feel the shattering of each pane of glass, am lacerated by every shard, feel the mortar breaking up—one brick separating from another.

I'm astonished by my own grief—what did I care? Hadn't I wanted to see the whole thing destroyed in the first place? "Dogma—schools—gone!" was the battle cry. Begin again from scratch this time. Start over. Make it new. Challenge everything. Follow nothing but the promptings of the unconscious. Give birth to the dream world. Tear down the house. Wake everybody up.

And yet here I am, bedridden, in physical pain, as if what they are pulling down from the inside is my own body, my bones groaning, breaking apart.

How strange it is to long for those old corridors and washrooms—the smell of spirits and soap and damp wool—grimy winter light through the windows. To ache for this physical structure that once symbolized both freedom and oppression to me—as if one longed for the Bastille, so one could keep storming it.

What kind of nostalgia is this?

Now there is nothing to tear down in my mind. That may be the real grief—losing something solid in the world that I can hate.

Did I hate the École des beaux-arts? Not really, though I sometimes resented it for being provincial, for not being the École du meuble in Montreal, or everything I imagined having such vitality in New York and then in Paris.

It was always happening elsewhere—the exhibitions, the manifestos. Here in Quebec City, we suffered the small aftershocks, never the earthquake. And it was the devastation of an earthquake I desired. I felt doomed to be forever far, far from the epicentre of anything but my own mind.

So I began there and returned to it again and again, trying to live the ideas of the *Refus Global*.

Letting the dream lead me. Dreaming a new world into being.

What would Theo have thought of *la crise d'Octobre?*

The FLQ murder one of the men they've taken hostage. The government invokes the War Measures Act. Soldiers everywhere. As if this were the revolution we dreamed of in 1948.

Vive le Québec libre!

Vive la révolution québécoise!

Vive le Front de libération du Québec!

"Du règne de la peur soustrayante nous passons à celui de l'angoisse."

From the reign of debilitating fear we pass to that of anguish.

No, the burnt umber will not do. Not upside down or right side up. In fact, I no longer remember how I began it. None of it is right. Layers and layers of smeared shit and menstrual blood.

I don't even bother scraping it off. I simply turn it to the wall and walk out.

Back again the next day. A blank canvas. Pastel colours. Raw linen between the swipes of paint. Light. Air. Breath.

No. Not that either. I take the canvas off the easel.

I smoke and pace and drink wine, trying to avoid looking at old work that hangs and leans up against things all around me.

Five o'clock and still no decision. I'm paralyzed. No light. No air. I no longer want to breathe. I want the stone on my chest to press it all out of me. Everything expelled from the body, forcibly, just before it dies.

I pull out the burnt umber, make gashes in the thick drying paint—fill them with mauve, yellow ochre. White. Press the light back in. Pull the dark out from behind.

Many years later, I go to see Riopelle's large new paintings at the Musée des beaux-arts.

Thirty canvases assembled on three walls, one wall cutting the room on the diagonal. They are vast and filled with maniacal energy. He is my age. How has he managed it?

How am I to read it? Where does it begin? Forwards, backwards, then I am lost.

I cannot make out the whole story.

Not a story at all.

It's as if all the events happened at once—as if all the images came at once. So I am forced to move back and forth. At every moment it is a new painting. It insists itself on me like a nightmare—recurring.

Memory.

Beyond memory.

Images set loose from every association.

Spirit birds—circles—portals—blood—moons.

Ferns, mushrooms, nails, bolts, fan blades, an oar—the things of this world floating alongside the things of the next. One reality alongside the other. The seen and the unseen on the same canvas.

Broken-necked herons, string, chicken wire.

Smaller birds rising in flight, then caught, splayed, pinned against the canvas, and outlined with spray paint.

The spectre of a gull, its red heart pierced by an arrow, compels me to step away, then to step closer.

It's as though I'd painted it myself, come across it in my studio after a long absence, forgotten about it entirely.

L'Hommage à Rosa Luxemburg. He painted it for his American lover after she died. It is full of a howling grief, and I cannot remain standing in the face of it.

Images scrambled out of order. Yet everything is there.

Our story, after all.

In a secret language—hieroglyphs from the future.

And I have grown unspeakably old.

So this is the world I am leaving: forsythia, willow trees budding—cherry blossoms floating through the air—jonquils, pansies, a time before the tulips, the earth softening, snow fields receding. The young walk, wrapped in one another's arms, stop to kiss mid-pavement. Shoppers and office workers separate and converge around them like water around rocks.

Today I forget that there is torture, avarice, and murder in the world, or death itself, the way one usually thinks about it, as though dying were as simple as stepping around young lovers and vanishing into thin air, slipping quietly out of one's skin with no effort at all.

And who's to say it isn't?

Today I can believe that it may well be … as easy as that.

Theo wanted to make a kite, *un cerf-volant*, with lights to fly at night. He said it would be a new star in the sky. A flying serpent. A dragon. He set about with sticks and painted paper, an elaborate Chinese lantern, a long tail with rags. It was astonishingly beautiful—mauve and red and yellow—but cumbersome, and I couldn't imagine it ever actually flying.

On a windy September evening near sunset, we took it to the fields between the convent and the mental hospital in Charlesbourg. We lit the kerosene holder with five different wicks he had rigged in the centre.

I held the kite lantern high above my head and began to run, fearing that the flames would go out.

"Lâche-le!" he cried. *"Laisse-le voler!"*

I tried to let it go, but I was afraid the wind would not pick it up.

"*Encore une fois.*"

I tried again. I stopped to catch my breath. "*J'n'en peux plus!*"

"*Essaye! Fais un effort!*"

I took off at a run once again, ran hard enough that I felt the burn in my thighs, and this time I decided to let go, no matter what.

I felt the kite lift out of my hands—a strong gust of wind had caught it—and for a moment I imagined being borne skyward with it.

Now it was Theo running, wildly, shouting in earnest.

"*Monte! Lève-toi, là, le con!*"

Out of breath, hands on my knees, I looked up and watched it rise—dip—and then rise and rise again.

"*Theo! Tu l'as fait! Il vole!*"

The kite stopped in midair. It shone brightly for a moment, and then burst into flames, falling at first in slow motion and then faster, with more and more smoke as its tail.

We ran over to where it had landed and stamped the fire out with our feet so it wouldn't ignite the dry stalks of wheat.

"*Une étoile filante,*" said Theo. "*Mais une étoile, quand même.*"

A falling star.

But a star, nonetheless.

ACKNOWLEDGEMENTS

My thanks to the staff of the Musée national des beaux-arts du Québec and the archivists and reference librarians at the Université Laval for their research assistance.

Many thanks to my first readers: Monica Wood, Stephen Boyd, Caroline Lamothe, James Tyler Irvine, and Alain-Michel Rocheleau.

A deep bow to Nina Shoroplova my editor, and to proofreader Rebecca Coates.

And thank you, Glenn Madsen, Ruth Payne, Patricia Baldwin, Ingunn & Michael Kemble, Freda Pagani & Jim Carruthers, for your generous friendship and support. Thank you, VIFF, VJFF, DOXA, The Arts Club, The Cultch, the students and faculty of Studio 58, the former Capilano College and the *Capilano Review*, booksellers like Emilie Dierking Joyce at Pulp Fiction, and everybody at Book Warehouse on Broadway and on Main Street. Thank you, Walter Quan for your enthusiastic support and your tireless work for arts in British Columbia. And to fellow cultural workers such as Trilby Jeeves, Mia Weinberg, Yokiko Onley, Tom Carter, Eve Lazarus, Janie Chang, Carol Condruk, Kevin Spenst, and Craig Addy—and many others, for your audacity, heart, courage, and determination to cultivate community in Vancouver no matter what the odds.

A special thanks for the ongoing work of the Benedictine Sisters in Nanaimo and the community of faith that has grown up around the chapel at the Bethlehem Centre, as well as at St. Paul's Anglican, Or Shalom, St. Mark's Parish, SoulStream, and the Threshold Society.

And to David Avalon, Sequoia Thom Lundy, David Hoe, John Neffenger, Achille Gardelini, Elfi & Gary Dillon Shaw, Leslie Ross, Rolf Reynolds, Keith Brydges, Philip Steeves, Will Tessier, James Clare, and Don Blythe for your patience, friendship, and good humour.

ALSO BY ALFRED DEPEW

The Melancholy of Departure

Wild & Woolly: A Journal Keeper's Handbook

A Wedding Song for Poorer People

About the Author

Alfred DePew has taught at the University of Vermont, the University of New Hampshire, the Maine College of Art, the Salt Center for Documentary Studies, and Haystack Mountain School of Crafts. He currently serves on the faculty of the Center for Right Relationship. He lives in Vancouver, BC, where he maintains a private practice in leader development, spiritual direction, professional supervision, evolutionary astrology, and dream work.

He may be reached through his website: alfreddepew. com/contact-me.

www.ingramcontent.com/pod-product-compliance
Lightning Source LLC
Chambersburg PA
CBHW021024120726
47905CB00009B/3169